Sanctuary

Other books by the author:

Prose
Beneath the Visiting Moon
The Almost Child
Sorry Days are Over

Poetry
The Green Dancers
The Burial Tree
And Suddenly This
From the White Room
Somewhere There Are Trains
Falconer
Last Days of the Eagle
Mornings of Snow
Figures and Masks
The Mind and Dying of Mister Punch
Stone Moon Poems
Return to the Abode of Love.
Replies for My Quaker Ancestors
Three Meeting Houses
Village Poems
A Banquet for Rousseau
A Romanian Round
The All Night Orchestra
The Rain Children
Turtle Mythologies
Bosnia

Education
The Gifted Child at School (Editor)

Anthology
An Idea of Bosnia (Editor)

SANCTUARY
David H.W. Grubb

SANCTUARY
First edition 1997
© David H.W. Grubb
All rights reserved
ISBN 1 900152 18 5

Cover art © Andi Sapey
Design by Neil Annat

Published by
Stride Publications
11 Sylvan Road, Exeter
Devon EX4 6EW

The idea of eternal return is a mysterious one

Milan Kundera

In time one mingles the fact of any message with the fiction
of one's interpretation of it.

David Wheldon, *The Course of Instruction*

For Beverly

1

He lay, gasping, clutching with filthy fingers the floorplanks of the tree house, praying that he was safe, that it would not suddenly rain, that he could not be seen from the ground.

Where was Thomas? Down there somewhere, hunting him, perhaps tiring a little, perhaps unsure. Was climbing into a tree cheating? As he lay there, regaining breath but hardly composure, Lucian wondered that he had not slipped, had slowly made it gripping the branches and using the unexpected nails driven in at intervals years ago. It had been if not exhilarating somehow compulsive. It had been a real test, the best of tests; physical and mental and totally unplanned. Suddenly he thought of the mad man of Antioch, Simeon, living on top of his pillar (or was it a tower?) and preaching to the human ants far beneath.

The thought made him look about. Was there something more meaningful here? Was there a revelation? Or was it to be appallingly ordinary? 'Priest caught in tree house. Local fire team called out. Minor injuries and a short stay in the cottage hospital!'

It was wonderfully quiet. He could see the rectory roof, the winding drive, the beginnings of the village, but he was mostly conscious of being within the greenness of it, within huge tree territory, between heat of a May day and this huge independence of boughs: majestic cedar arms, poplars folding and unfolding in the wind. The wind was somehow different here, smelling of bark. The tree house itself was still sturdy, God be praised. Two sides had fallen away but somebody had been up here to carve a recent date. Probably village boys. They were always in the rectory gardens, searching for conkers or coming to scoop frogspawn from the small lake or using one of the sheds to smoke in. For many years now Lucian had pretended not to see them. He wasn't going to chase them off and risk abuse at his age. All that had gone. They might as well enjoy the ruined estate whilst it was here.

Was Thomas still down there or had he given up? Lucian slowly brought up his knees and knelt to look over and down. It really was a long way down. Give it a few minutes longer and then he'd attempt the descent.

A sort of daftness but it made him smile. What other aged priests got up to such innocent games with their grandsons? Did any of his fellow clergy even dream of such fun? Not simply hide and seek; far more elaborate games relating to Navajo and Hopi and Sioux and hunting. Lying flat on your belly and parting the grasses. Every time Thomas came they went out, leaving the adults to talk, the ritual family gossip.

It had begun with more ordinary activities, hunting for moths in overgrown hedges and trying to find old cobbled pathways and touring the walled-in kitchen garden to see what was left in butts and searching for frogs, spiders, hedgehogs. Thomas always asking about what it had once been like, wanting to hear again about the garden fetes and tennis afternoons and the strange ritual of bowls and who had planted the Yucca and about the discovery of the bronze palitave now residing in Exeter museum. When they were inside the rectory Thomas was quiet, respectful, a different child. Once he and his grandfather had escaped it was all much easier, it opened out, reality rushed in different directions always capable of surprising Lucian and giving him new life, glorious senses of hope, flourishes of the almost forgotten.

But the boy had gone now, there was no sign of him far down in the green; no noise of the hunter, no call, no signs.

Lucian had to consider the descent. Would it be any easier? Or was he going to spoil the adventure, make a fool of himself? 'Old man rescued by local fireman. Told not to climb trees again. Parishioners worry about senile priest', etc.

Hadn't there been a rope here once? When it was built there must have been something to make it easier, a more logical way to begin, a few more nails strategically placed to get off the deck and down to the first large bough.

He recalled Richard and Sidney and other boys building it. A flurry of images to do with the boys; firework parties, a rowing boat, cricket matches, the energy required to keep up with it all, the wisdom required to ignore it, the gradual separation of skills and interests, the harsher years of criticism and disagreement, the going of own ways, and gradually the reconciliations, adulthood, conversations, rewards of a totally different kind.

He began to work his way down, at first legs dangling and then finding the places, beginning to trust himself, noticing now some cuts and bruises on his hands, hearing his breaths in short rushes again, a little fear within the exhilaration.

He was aware of the smell of bark again, the dense juices of trees and high branches and hidden life forms; an abode that one normally merely sensed at special moments but so rarely participated in, inhabited.

And then he fell, not awkwardly and tossed from bough to bough and not with a dramatic scream or any sort of shout. He fell clear and in silence like a large sack, something discarded, straight to the ground.

Thomas was there to see it, or at least the last part of it; his grandfather Lucian falling as if from the sky, from a tree, from somewhere which must have been the place where he had been hiding.

Thomas had himself played the wise game; wait in a hidden place for the creature you are hunting to forget you or assume that you have passed by. It could take a long time. One could become quite lonely.

In the heart of that May afternoon he had initially waited for sounds. His grandfather had taught him that; "let your ears act as eyes". Then he'd done some more moving about on his belly but it was almost too hot for that. Then he had simply waited. In the dense green, about five hundred yards from the house, with the small lake behind him. He'd been lying there, sometimes hearing a moorhen, watching small butterflies, thinking of his parents and the way his grandfather sometimes smelt of old books and how he wished there was a dog. And then he saw to his left grandfather Lucian failing from nowhere, at speed, and grunting as he hit the ground.

Was it part of the game? Was he supposed to creep up on the body? Might his grandfather suddenly spring up and whoop? Was he playing at some sort of eagle, or prehistoric flying beast?

Thomas decided to stop playing. He stood up and ran across to the body. By this time Lucian was sitting up. "Thomas; aha Thomas," he said; "Thomas, I think you've just witnessed a miracle. Help me up, will you?"

And as they walked back to the rectory Thomas heard his grandfather saying, "Now I think we'll just keep it a secret. We won't tell the others, see. It might spoil our fun. No, we won't tell anyone; you see, they might think I'm a bit too old to be failing from the tops of trees."

At high tea, amongst the usual clatter of images and sounds, the bright etiquette of family life, Lucian was content to assimilate, survive. After all, that is what he'd learnt to do as a priest these many years. Whilst his soul yearned to reveal the divine, the terrible truths of supernatural spasms, he trained himself to listen to the ordinary, protecting the commonplace because unworldly truths might terrify. His job was to cloak reality.

"And what did you get up to with your mad grandpa?" his wife, Paula, was asking Thomas, whilst Richard, Lucian's son, winked at his wife Maureen. Richard as always was consuming large quantities of cake, tackling the high tea in reverse as if he were never going to eat again. Maureen on the other hand ate slowly and very little, constantly fussing over Thomas who to Lucian's relief was not going to give the game away.

"We had a look at the lake, then we had a game of guessing the names of the trees, and then we did some hunting things," he replied.

Paula carved some more ham. " Ah yes, that would explain all that moss and green mess on your grandpa's trousers. What a pity he can't act sensibly like men of his own age. Richard, now that you've done my cake to death how about some ham?"

Lucian spent a great deal of this meal waiting for the worst to happen. Nothing too dramatic for nobody had seen him actually falling. No parishioner was likely to run in and give the secret away. No interference from Prebble the verger for once. What he feared was a sudden stab of pain from just about any part of his anatomy. He had, after all, fallen from a considerable height. Babies might bounce but not grandfathers. At any moment part of his back might send a burning signal to his brain or more simply seize up. Then he'd have to say something about the fall.

But what would he say? Were they going to have one of those daft scenes with Paula scolding him, Thomas holding his hand, Richard lecturing him and trusty Maureen getting the doctor on the phone. "Ah yes; is that you doctor; well my father-in-law fell out of a tree two hours ago and...".

But so far no pain. Hands a bit bruised but he'd brushed his nails well and slapped on some hand cream. (Strange stuff. Did Paula still use it regularly and how did one get the container thing to deposit just the right amount?) A quick inspection of clothes. Brush down the trousers and shake the pullover free of bark dust and moss. Feeling guilty like a boy. Shards of memory, things from years ago, even the odour of the school dormitory, before the sound of the gong for high tea.

Richard was talking now. A publisher of computer things. Nothing wrong with that but it restricted them somehow. No chance to talk man to man about something of common interest. If it had been antiques or even something to do with sport or country life, but there it was.

Sidney? If he had lived would there have been an opening there or would Sidney have become the bank manager, a technology person, or as Paula had always said 'something political'. Whatever did she mean?

And later the farewells. Thomas hugging his grandpa, an exchanged wink, Lucian slipping him something to add to his pocket money, promises to Paula to see them again soon, the company car making the Polo look shabby, and Maureen thanking Lucian for being such a super grandpa. Whatever illness, frailty, Maureen was meant to have, she was a quiet comfort to Lucian; getting on so well with her reassured him. No doubt Richard received some good reports. It hadn't all died with Sidney. Somehow there was some sort of bridge to Richard and one day it might be used.

And now the big house was empty again. Paula would switch on the radio or the record player and if pains suddenly came on Lucian would need to howl above the romantic din. Then she'd go into the parts of the huge garden that were still cared for and to end up talking to the yucca, a mystery plant that had last flowered in 1938. There were still people who came to see it hoping to be lucky enough to see it bloom. They had apparently read up on other delights in the rectory garden and were to be disappointed. When Lucian retired it was highly unlikely that a new rector would take over this property. They would probably combine several parishes and offer him a smaller and more economical place. And somebody like Richard would come along and buy up the house to convert it. It would become a private hotel or nursing home. It might even be pulled down. Paula always said some way-out religious community should take it over and 'let the light in'.

Lucian was not inclined to attack the garden and rediscover its glories. His predecessor had done so, operating virtually a small holding with ducks and Chinese geese and pigs and a deep litter system. His son had even had a rowing boat for the lake. But eventually he had given up. It required several men to keep it up. It had all been a hopeless adventure and the villagers had not appreciated a farmer rector. They grumbled that he had no time to visit them, or that he was making financial profit from the land and that this should have been given to the church. When he put sheep into the churchyard to keep the grass down that was seen as the last straw. They sent letters to the archdeacon who was finally forced to take legal action. To the archdeacon's surprise and horror the rector stood up for private enterprise and this little squabble was taken up by the press and finally an ecclesiastical court sat to settle the dispute. Having lost this battle the rector attempted to make ends meet in other ways. There was great activity in the orchard and in the kitchen garden followed by ploughing up parts of the formal garden and the cellars became some sort of mushroom farm. The rector visited his parishioners even less and rumours began again. The rector was seldom seen during the week. His wife and son were seen driving delivery vans. The rectory looked even more like a farm. There were more visits by local reporters and then a suggestion of financial scandal and finally another ecclesiastical court deprived the man of his living.

When two years later Lucian took over, all that was required by the villagers and churchwardens was that he acted in an acceptable manner, preaching the orthodox message, visiting the young and sick, pottering about the parish, letting his wife run the Mothers' Union. They wanted no more newspaper reporters, no goings on, no progressive ideas, no young men keen for advancement, and if the new man got up to anything at all then Prebble would let the authorities know. In the two pubs and in the farmhouses this was understood. Whoever became churchwarden in the coming years was hardly relevant so long as the people who really mattered were clear about this.

Had Lucian known much about this, the detail, he might never have accepted the living; Paula most certainly would not. But neither of them had come to Devon to challenge anything. This was likely to be their final parish.

The boys would be able to enjoy a country living in the school holidays in their late teenage years, before college or university or whatever it was going to be. The overgrown garden and the large house were not seen as a challenge but an essential change from city work, the endless struggle to bring in money for church repairs and the upkeep of church halls, the civic duties required in Tunbridge and before that in Birmingham. Paula wanted the boys to know something else of England and Lucian had already suffered one breakdown. He didn't seek preferment within the church, simply some space to breathe and be his own man. His great grandfather had ministered to a Devon village; there was possibly something in the blood to help him. And if the main requirement was to visit the people in their homes and listen to them he sensed that he could carry out his duties very well. He would serve these people in a quiet way, a simple festival of listening and fundamental preaching; some time for village history perhaps, an opportunity to work up his collection of antiquarian books; not a place of challenges or miracles or inquisitions. A quiet and English faith. If his small story of a Devonshire village were ever taken up by a publisher then he might regard that as more significant than any book of sermons or the one or two hymns that had already been published. A token of his quiet observations, his listening to essential signals, something to hand on to any grandchildren. He was no Abraham, no Moses, at best a winter prophet with a sound sense of the seasons and other people's dreams.

That night, however, he could not sleep. Perhaps he should talk it over with Paula. She would surely see some bruises or notice his hands. The left one had swollen now. But there truly were no other signs; not a single bruise to show and no stiffness.

Paula was indeed more than surprised to wake up in the early hours to find Lucian out of bed and attempting to bend over and touch his toes.

"What on earth are you up to?" she exclaimed. "Lucian, do you know what time it is?"

"I couldn't sleep. I was defying my age. I was wondering when I last touched my toes."

"At two-thirty in the morning!"

"At any time at all," he said and he wondered if she could smile at this.

Would they now drift, each one alone, each capsule of reality gently rocking, touching sometimes, yet a world of its own?

Would she, taking up her book, really enter another world, really leave his?

Would he, seated in the white wicker chair (his grandfather's and now badly painted over by him) be able to talk to her. And how should be begin? I My dear, I've been keeping something from you. Today I fell from the top of a tree, landed on the ground with nothing to break the fall and suffered no harm... no harm at all ... unbelievably.'

But Paula had taken up a book, another world, a graceful escape, until she re-entered countless necessary dreams.

Lucian stared at his toes, his hands, his perfect nails. Sidney had had his mother's hands, Wittingham hands. He had seen the same hands in Ireland and in the households of American cousins in the U.S.A.

Lucian, left to float within his own knowing, heard the church clock strike three. He momentarily saw the face of his dead son, the church clock face, an imagined moon, an owl face, a stone lion at Delos, a cathedral bell. The images fled. Lucian, given time to think, could not think clearly, could not define his good fortune. Well well; what are we coming to? Falling through air from a great height with damage to neither limb nor mind. Ah; but one is not sure of the latter. One cannot simply let it go at that! A lifetime of reflecting upon miracles and prophecies of miracles and the virtues of innocence and yet when it happens in one's own realty (what an odd phrase and yet so often one shared other people's concepts of reality having yielded one's own space and place) one refuses the dazzling energy, the opportunity to escape the normal, the possibility of laws defied. And who does a priest speak to? His wife, his son, his God? Certainly not the latter! If one fails to get a satisfactory response from a direct line one might never pick up the receiver again.Too close, too challenging. Would one rather risk God's growl or God's laughter? "I dropped you from that bough to shake you to a new purpose, a new recognition, a fresh reality. You have grown old, grown old making me an old God; I let you fall and not feel the pain because that was the only way to leave you wordless, listening, aware, not rushing to cover up the gap with codes or explanations. At least that worked, you must agree. But now what is it you want to do, I must prevent you from doing? Don't hold up your intellect to shield you from my light. For heaven's sake listen to me!"

God's groan. God's grunt. God's game. And if one doesn't tackle it this way, how? I fall from a tree, from a height, at sixty three, and should be dead. But no pain, not even a bruise. All the scratches and bruises were done on the way up. So now I sit within this mental fidget finding not consolation but a drum beat of disturbance, some sort of recoiling, something more like despair to be still alive!

A quick thought for Lazarus. A momentary consideration for the astigmatics. Although no miracle, no actual divine reordering, at best a cheat, a disordering; but why, oh why?

Lucian in his three a.m. wide awake conversation with God and himself, or seated on the toilet, or sluggish in his bath, or waiting for dreams. Lucian unable to cry 'hold, enough' and babble it all out to Paula. Unable even to record it in his dearly beloved diary. Not a word of it (not even thanks) in his prayers. Might it be the beginning of another breakdown? Not a chance. Never felt better. Then what in heaven's name was it come knocking at his door? And with what persistence!

2

Lucian's parish possessed hills, the edges of moors, open land and woods, springs, streams and marshes, and where old buildings now stood there had been earlier ones. Within fashions, fables and things forgotten most things were revised, refashioned: the history of the village was resurrections.

The annals of the village recorded the drowning of the farmer and his son in the river Exe in May 1789. They had been on business and had crossed the river on horseback. During the day a heavy storm raised the water level and that evening attempting to cross again the darkness had deceived them. Both men and the horse were swept by the current downstream. The horse got to land half a mile down but the man and his son were drowned. The boy's body was taken from the weir on May 31st. The father was not found until June the 7th. Both bodies now lie in the village churchyard: William aged twelve and John aged forty five. But the annals do not carry the humanity, the horror, the histories of such people. These are dried up facts. They lie down in musty texts. They don't sound out from mighty tapestries. Only stories of ghosts will bring them back.

The swindler, impostor John Hatfield had lived in the village in 1801. He deserted leaving his wife and two very young children. When in 1803 he was convicted and hanged there is evidence of the rector of the parish trying to assist the woman and her infants. But the screams of doubt, the pain of folly, the harsh future to be faced; where are they recorded? It is now as if that woman had disappeared from this planet.

Blizzards, the church tower blowing down, the village being cut off by gales, epidemics; these are shades, phrases, common enough to escape comment. The 1901 census: male – 156, female 176, total – 332. Where did their conversations go, their fidelities, their foibles, their fun? Was there fun?

In 1944 a large bomb was dropped in the parish. It fell in afield of oats. Evidently it was jettisoned and had been intended for Bristol. It happened about 3 a.m. and gave a loud report. The measurements of the crater were 40 feet width, 129 feet circumference, 12 feet 8 inches deep. These are roughly the same dimensions as the crater at Buckingham Palace. The total casualties – one field mouse.

And, so far apart, another drowning. Two girls aged 14 and 13, whilst bathing in a pool below the weir. This took place in front of their mothers who could not rescue them. The pool, eight feet deep, had been created by the winter floods. Do the ghosts of John and William know, sense it? Is there something deep reflected there, in some parts of the river?

The people who have passed on become stones, memorial benches, windows, bells, tarnished texts, costumes, customs, stories. And their places change; their houses and huts and lanes and paths. Orchards become small estates. Mansions become museums or hotels. The shape of fields, hedges, even hillsides change. The way people speak changes. What they would say changes. And our current babble buries the other voices, the past deeper and deeper. The sound and then the sights and then the dream of them disappears. When we no longer reach into their dreams their history is dead. The daylight and then the night drowns. And finally the silence prevents their being there. Every trace of their being goes out.

And so May Day, on the first Saturday in May if not on the 1st of May, designed now with the tourists in mind and the availability of young mothers and the men who make up the band rather than to observe a speeding pulse of the sun, of the green blood of nature.

Lucian thankful that the traditional church fete had been dropped in his predecessor's time but always attending (looking for the ghosts of Richard and Sidney) and Paula always working away on some silly stall or sideshow.

At ten a.m. it began with a procession from the church, through the main street, past the school, down to the village hall and ending at the playing fields by the hall.

Lucian was required to appear, dressed in his robes, and the choir that had grown too old to sing from the top of the tower sang what many were surprised to be told was a carol. Lucian then orated a poem specially created for the occasion by Hilda Morrison or Patricia Morrison who as sisters were sole teachers at the village primary school. On paper the poem looked trite but Lucian made the best of it whether the sun blessed the occasion or he had to yell into a sprightly wind. Over the years he had actually done this in hail, in torrents, in a thunderstorm twice and once in snow.

After the oration the procession slowly moved off. The youngest children led, posies in hands, flowers round their heads, followed by some young musicians, then a section of the band and finally the May Queen hopefuls. This group of nubile beauties also carried posies and wore garlands in their hair but were in every way singularly different from the rest of the procession. The prize money, the free weekend in London and the opportunity to parade in front of the local lads enticed at least a dozen hopefuls each year. They wore their skirts very short.

Many years ago the choir and church banners would have augmented this gaudy throng, but nowadays they could not sing to a band or compete with the catcalls or the roars from motor bikes. Lucian also no longer joined. The choir and banners and priest were no longer called for. Better to bow out gracefully and be glad to be asked to recite a poem. Settle for this and don't risk ridicule. Don't drag the church through more ludicrous and confused images, vestiges of history, warped historical tapestries. Settle for Hilda's or Patricia's pretty nonsense and then get onto your bike and see where the procession's got to.

Flags, bunting, balloons along the school railings. All the village out in this year's sun. A few remembering Victory parades. A few recalling coronation street parties. Union Jacks and Stars and Stripes and a hardly noticed Japanese flag. Past the school and through the central car park and past the pubs, already open. Then on to the village hall and the playing fields where the rest of the band had congregated and the May Pole already stood in place and a throne for the new May Queen.

By twelve-thirty the crowd had swollen, the pubs were full, the hall was packed with hungry locals and visitors queuing for salad lunches and soup and pies. The hall always smelling of tea bags. Full or empty, summer or winter, fête or theatricals, the odour of tea bags was constantly there. And there was also a sense of something; of amateur endeavour, of prayers and parades, of clubs and groups, of card players and dramatics and speeches. The heavy stage curtains, the stacked chairs and trestle tables, the tea urns, the currant cake, the jostle of dialogue, the memorial plaques and faded formal photographs in fragile frames; these all somehow stuck in time, the place itself lodged in space. It swallowed the present and made things somehow less than serious, not in any way trivial but less than perfect. Perhaps village halls all share this failure to be truly serious, relevant, beloved.

At two-thirty the May Queen was named, the band played its terrible music as if all the world wanted to dance, men bowled for prizes which were never pigs, Punch and Judy terrified the extremely young, the fortune teller told expensive lies, the May Pole became a candy bar again and again, the local lads lay down to get seriously drunk.

Lucian mingled with tourists, locals, layabouts. As a party May Day in the village was superior to some of the other celebrations. November 5th bonfire crowds in the same recreation field with mulled wine in the village hall and hot dogs and that amazing stench of dead autumn. And in high summer the primary school fête, smaller and a little less attractive and purposeful each year. And then a village wedding: everybody joining in as if they were close relatives, the massive blooming bouquets, the unruly noise and sense of almost tribal expectation, a blending of what was expected and what was half feared in the polite but nervous speeches and the crude, crackling jokes. Lucian was always aware of this mixture of the blessed and suggestive kindly kindled in these graces and disgraces.

By three p.m. the sky had dulled and by four o'clock the rain was falling like old lace. The band persisted for a while, the May Queen and her attendants gently rotting on their platform, rouge running down their faces, posies slowly turning into dripping mop heads. The Morris Dancers were the first to call it a day, then the handbell ringers, and finally the primary school children abandoned the May Pole dancing, red mud splattered up their legs.

From the hall where teas were being served to hundreds, individuals made dashes to the car park, or to their cottages. The drains emitted red slush, the bunting leaked grey, the flags clung rigid to their poles.

It was too early for the pubs to open. The dance wouldn't start before eight. The hall began to reek of damp bodies, ancient tea urns, tea towels, damp dogs, the aroma of old and almost past it potted plants. A smell of damp wood and rotting paper. The odour of rotten carpets, of beer bottle crates, of wicker chairs. Laughter from porches and the bus shelter and the telephone kiosks bursting with children smoking. Occasional bursting balloons. Once or twice even a firework.

Lucian saw the faces of villagers and strangers. He even knew some of the locals from their rear views. 'Titch' Mabley who was a bit simple and sometimes assisted Prebble with churchyard work. Mike Smith who exactly a year ago had broken down with grief; "all my life has gone out, all gone out you see". Sylvia Thompson who thought her cottage was haunted. The entire Williams family. all seven of them. who had driven in from the moor in a fiendish jeep. Frank Evans and Sally Evans who lived as husband and wife but who were in fact brother and sister, and Tammy their child. And those others, ordinary folk whom Lucian knew were part of the village community but not churchgoers. Faces from the lanes, from the shops, from the pub. Faces that are passed in all seasons and who recognised Lucian as the rector.

Faces that would appear in the pubs that night, voices raised, or faces behind cottage curtains whispering secrets and regrets and solaces. The young folk at the dance letting out war whoops and abusive yells and late, late that night howling out from the orchards and further fields. The drunken calls, the whistles, the revving and roar of motor cycles and small vans, Christopher and Billy Norrish hurling their tractor round the bends. The rain still falling, flaying, fashioning damp ruins, contracting the sounds and crowds and purposes so that even a closed cottage door was suggestive. The old gravestones in the churchyard rearing up like amazing, ancient, impossible fish, the church itself like some necessary stone whale.

The rain chases across old stone, lichen, names and texts, staining and staining, burying and drowning again and again. The very old are here, and those who left a great deal behind, or those who did not live long enough to create in their own image.

3

At one time there were at least eight farms within the village which was almost self-supporting. In the last quarter of the 19th century there was a vicar, a solicitor, a cowkeeper and victualler, a vet, a cider merchant, a postmaster, a poulterer, a butcher, a wheelwright, a blacksmith, a shoemaker, a fellmonger, a stonemason and small manufacturers. The Board School was erected in 1876 with accommodation for 75 children. The least changed and one of the oldest buildings was the Church House. The earliest recorded vicar died in 1321. Later vicars died of the Plague or of the Black Death. One was deprived of the living. Another served for as long as thirty three years. In the ancient church there was a 13th century window and a 13th century statue of the Blessed Virgin. In the porch stocks for two persons still stood. The lych gate was the oldest dated wooden lych gate in England.

For Peggy Newson the village historian it was not the artefacts and remains that stimulated most interest, it was the idea of what these people might have been. She did not see history as mirrors or windows but as messages and looked for small signals in the activities of people rather than statements from their buildings.

She was currently researching hunting and hawking and an almost frantic destruction of vermin.

Hunting and hawking have been popular sports in Devonshire for many hundreds of years. Wolf-hunting and boar-hunting were necessities until as late as the fifteenth century, and the pursuit of the stag upon horseback was practised as early as the time of the Normans. Before the Conquest there is evidence to suggest that the chase was conducted on foot, and consisted rather in trapping and lying in wait for the deer than in capturing them after exhausting their strength by putting their powers of endurance and fleetness of foot to the proof.

The privilege of hunting beasts of chase was reserved for the king throughout the Middle Ages, and to such nobles, clergy, and others to whom licence or grant was made to hunt in certain forests or stretches of land. It was a privilege, which down to the time of Elizabeth was deemed to be the sport only of kings and worthy personages, and not for men of mean calling or condition.

At such moments, with such information to hand (and actually in her hand), Peggy Newson wondered what she was really doing. She wasn't an historian, she wasn't interested in sociology; what was the term that might apply to someone who observed but not at a distance, who not only pondered but sometimes intervened? ' Romantic ' wasn't correct or strong enough, it wasn't a single poetic view. It was too disturbed for that. "History is not a philosophy" her brother had once said, disturbed by her ideas about Mayan customs; you muddle the impulses and lo and behold you offer us prepositions'.

Yet 'men of mean calling or condition' were still part of it. They saw it, heard about it, expected it to happen in their territory. They made some small profit from it and made sense or nonsense of it. People who were living within the major events could not be considered as peripheral.

When nearly all the royal forests were disafforested in James I's reign, and during the succeeding century when England was fully occupied with civil war, and the rise and fall of kings and dynasties, hunting passed through a lean time, and various laws were passed for the destruction of vermin, and the protection of agricultural land from 'noyfull fowles and vermin.'

About the middle of the eighteenth century we come to surer ground, and both stag-hunting and foxhunting commenced to settle down and develop as popular sports of the county, and the breeding of hounds and horses for the hunt was taken up eagerly upon many farms and estates.

She wondered about the other popular sports such as bull-baiting and cock-fighting, wrestling and cricket, football and fishing, shooting and snaring birds of all kinds. Did she see ancestors on the village green when the cricket match was on? Could she actually claim this? And when she saw prints of bull-baiting or cock-fighting why did she stare so much at the staring faces rather concentrating on the subjects of their stare?

Was there old blood in this, returning like ancient sap? Was it the same struggle? It was easier to see it as ritual, symbolism with lords and kings, but the bodies of common people could not so easily be dispossessed. The sources that came from ordinary cupboards and drawers and pockets were to her more 'possible' than treaties, tapestries, wisdoms.

Until the reign of Henry VIII farmers and landowners were free to kill the fox, and keep down vermin on their land as best they could. In 1532, in consequence of the innumerable number of rooks, crows, and choughs, it was enacted that each parish was to provide itself with a net for their destruction, to maintain it for ten years and to present it annually before the manor court steward. Two pence was to be paid for every twelve old crows, rooks, or choughs by the owner or occupier of the manor or land.

For the further destruction of 'Noyfull Fowles and Vermyn' and for the better preservation of grain, Queen Elizabeth in 1566 renewed and extended the above act to include all kinds of birds and other vermin. Each holder of land was assessed a yearly amount by the churchwardens, payable to the parish accounts, and by the churchwardens paid out as a reward to every person bringing before them once a month the heads or eggs of such vermin. The scale for such payments is of interest, as well as some of the bird-names then used:

For the heads of old crows. choughs. pyes or rookes   3 a 1d.

Ditto. young crows, ditto   6 a 1d.

For every six eggs of them, unbroken   6 a 1d.

For the heads of stares   12 a 1d.

Ditto, Martyn hawkes, busardes, and schagges   2d each.

Ditto, furskyttes and modeekyttes (Kites)   2d each.

Ditto camerats and ryngtales (hen harriers)   2d.each

For every two eggs of the above   1d.each

For the heads of irons or sprays (Ospreys)   4d.each

Ditto, woodwalls, jayes, or ravens -   1d.each

Ditto, of everie Byrde which is called the Kinges Fysher   1d.each

Ditto, for everie Byrde that devowreth the blowth of Fruite 1d.each

Ditto, of everie bullfynche	1d.each
Ditto, of everie foxe or gray -	12d.each
Ditto, of everie fitchere, polecatte, Wesell, or stote	1d.each
Ditto, of everie otter or Hedgehogge	2d.each
Ditto, of everie three rattes, or twelve myse (mice)	1d.
Ditto, of every moldewarpe or wante	1/2d.each

And here was something else, like looking at a very old mirror or hearing ancient music played in its original form, these ancestral terms and names coming back or out of time so that she could stand in her small room and speak them out loud: 'busardes' and 'schagges', 'furskyttes' and 'modeekyttes', of everie Byrde which is called the Kinges Fysher', 'for everie Byrde that devowreth the blowth of Fruite'. Such language came back like song in a winter garden.

But then. so often, as if a giant had entered such a place, to roll in wrath and panic and passion, a shock sprang back from the past.

The heads and eggs, after account had been taken of them, were to be burnt. consumed, or out in sunder before the churchwardens and their assessors. Often left lying about in the churchyard, where payment was made and sometimes nailed to the church door, the dogs of the neighbourhood found a splendid feeding ground and as a result the appointment of a new church officer called the 'Dogwhipper, became a necessity.

It was to her like a summer tide caught in sunset but bringing onto the sand not simply a ruin or rags but a drowned child. The money and passions roared in men's heads so that they sometimes killed massively.

Payments in some years are laboriously entered item by item, and in others in one lump sum. If the fixed scale was religiously adhered to in one years, in another the payments were irregular, and seem to have varied according to age, position, and sex of the slaughterer! Perhaps some exploits were deemed worthy of a higher honour, that is of a higher payment, on the analogy of war medals, than others. Some illustrations may be given:

1669. pd Mr. George Cockram's man for killing a Gee	01.01.00
1670. pd John Ward for killing of Jayes and Hoops	00.01.00
pd for killing 2 oupes	00.00.02
pd to severall psons for killings of 17teene hedgehoggs	00.02.10
1679. pd ffor woops, Jayes and a Gray	00.11.00
1696. pd for a ffox to Mr. Pulman's man	0. 0. 0

Evidently Mr. Pulman's man had had a good day's sport after this fox, for which, or perhaps on the strength of the story he told the churchwardens, he received five times as much as the usual payment!

The infrequency of such items of payment in the accounts suggest that either foxes were rare in this neighbourhood, or more probably that they were shot by the farmers, and the expense for their destruction not charged to the parish accounts.

Sometimes there were two claimants for joint action in killing a badger, or other animal, cf.

1673. Paid Thomas Alien, and Phillipp Shippard for killing a Graye	00.01.00
1694. Paid John Hooper & Mr Samuel Pulman for tenn hedgehoggs, and fower poule Catts	00.02.04

And for digging out fitch holes, the sum of fourpence each was paid.

pd unto Severall psons for Seventeen ffitchholes at 4d. a peece	00.05.08
pd unto Severall psons for Two & twenty hedghogs at 2d. a peece	00.03.04
pd unto Severall psons for Three & twenty Jays at 1 d. a peece	00.01.11

It seemed to her also that such actions were directly imitated by the young for the very worst of reasons. When it was a case of blood young children were always present; swinging on the legs of the straggling at the gallows or screaming at the bloody bears fighting off the dogs or roaring at the cock-fight, flushed with fear but immersed in the adult grip of guilt. Was this what she saw in the village today when a crowd of children surrounded a playground fight? Was this urge still there when a gang screamed after the village simpleton? Was there something there, clinging and grim, in the minds of the motor cycle gangs as they revved and roared. Even recently she had read of the police failing to prosecute men in Essex, men who were found at a badger sett, men who would normally take the badger back in the sack to set the dogs on it for sport. But in order to give the dogs a chance the badger was normally in some way maimed.

That the boys and girls of the parish frequently occupied themselves in the excitement (and sport?) of the vermin hunts is evidenced from a number of such entries as the following:

1706. pd Tho-, Marshalls maid for 5 hoopes	0.0.21/2
pd Mr. Dickes boy 4 hoopes	0.0.2
pd Mr. Sumpter's son 4 hoopes	0.0.2
pd Mr. Crosses boy 4 hoopes	0.0.2

That children should only have been paid half the proper price and the number of such items of payments to boys and maids this year suggests that the churchwardens had found a cheap way of saving the parish money.

Sometimes Peggy Newson regretted her single state, the lack of family, the silences that were a good part of her days. These words moving across the pages were an essential comfort, but that wasn't the word. In fact it was totally the wrong word. She sensed and then she knew that she was in fact moving from texts to dreams.

4

Prebble, faced with nettles, litter, rain damage caused by blocked gutters, things he found stuffed into the small collection box at the lych gate, grass that at this time of year could turn into a tide of green within two weeks, a cylinder mower that didn't work. "Titch" Mabley muttering and grumbling and spitting, a dead rat or two, another wedding coming up, two graves to dig, kept on thinking of God's silence. God was silence; it was as pure and simple as that. God was silence.

The font was silence, holy water passing through God's eternal light. Norman, ancient, square shaped, round topped. A stone of holy silences. Not babies, babble, crying, the stupid women who came to see their baby named. Water and holy light and the image of the cross pressed gently onto infant flesh. God's signature coming back to make the meaning real. The kiss of hope.

Cleaning it. Not scrubbing. Never damaging. Old Canon Robinson years ago using water he'd brought back from Bethlehem (out of a large green bottle). How could one clean where holy water had been? Mrs Balter using the consecrated water to put on her husband's grave. Never scrubbing. The font the first object meeting the eye (the mind) upon entering the church. God's light in the water, even His sound, His whisper to a child. Even for fat, stupid Annie Blazey and her twins. Two plump kids held screaming and kicking whilst parson Doyle (thirty years ago) tried to make himself heard, tried to get some sense in it, tried to get some order going, tried to make it sensible. And another time that silly man sent in when parson Doyle was dying, to baptise the triplets, bringing his dog into church. Always did that. Said he'd always done it in Dublin and didn't see why it was so wrong here. Lot of other stupid things he did as well. Different sort of God they had in Dublin, in Ireland, over there.

Prebble and Hilda White and Mavis Duke all working there, in the silence, cleaning. Polishing. Protecting. Preserving God's peace. Place of God. House of God. Territory that had to be protected from modern ideas and changes and abuse.

And in that silence (dusting, polishing, sweeping) the large tick tock and whish of the clock, the tap tap of the mechanism before it struck, the sense from inside of some enormous force gathering to strike out across the village and beyond, a sound of certainty, endurance, trust. Not a thing to be ignored. Not something crude. Nothing that came again and again by chance, accident, mistake.

Prebble at the pulpit with his polish and cloth and sense of serving. Hilda with the soft brushes and mop. Mavis (the youngest) with a tendency to hum a little, her polishing rags working on the brasses, bringing out the old gold behind and texts that nobody bothered to read any more.

Armigur Henricus cubat hoc sub semate Worthus
Worthus clarus avis secia trecina suis...

And in that silence (God's work, God's silence) Prebble with his sense of purpose and determination and need to protect.

There were so many who came to this place making it their own, putting down markers, working out territory. The way they dressed, the way they spoke, the way they observed, even their manner of praying. Dorothy and Daniel Smith clasping their hands in prayer and returning to their pews having received the sacrament hand in hand as if courtship were eternal. And yet during the week, in the shop, she was curt and bossy and he was constantly eyeing up Sally Gormley who assisted for a scandalously low wage. And Matthew Collins who always sat in the front, dressed in a dark blue suit which he wore summer and winter. Lingering over his amens as if God would remember his Sunday sound and forget how he had slowly starved his mother to death (locking her in the garden shed night after night). And once a year the British Legion coming with their flags and marchers. And once a year also the Mothers' Union filled the church with proud bosoms and patriotic pulsations. And once a year the Young Farmers came to modernise their concept of sun and oil and servitude. And once a year the students from Dean's College crowded in to start the academic year with a real trounce of tradition.

They all came, made their noise, caught onto the idea of God, winked at Him and passed on. Colonel Harrogate was no better, Doctor Pew was no better, the local solicitor and Thomas Child the bank manager were no better. They clocked in, made the special noises, acted out their pasts, made their marks, and Lucian Fairbrother acted out his part as all the rectors had before him. A small voice between the choirmaster and the choir and the congregation. Somebody who knew his place and accepted it. God's man within the limits of tradition and ritual and the appetite of the congregation.

Prebble had in all his years of service, through the incumbencies of no less than five rectors, never once imagined that without his own careful watch things might go terribly wrong. By this he did not mean a grave dug too shallow, or a funeral booked on the wrong day, or a wedding where the groom was too tanked up, or a christening where the names got mixed up, or the very embarrassing occasion when he personally had to add to the Christmas midnight communion wine with his sister's elderberry cordial. Prebble like many of his breed was constantly alert to avoid some sterner blasphemy. He had heard of drunken priests, priests who did things in the vestry to choir boys, priests who got ideas into their heads, priests who went over the top. It wasn't that uncommon. Perhaps it was being so isolated. not able to easily mingle with ordinary folk, always expected to be a cut above. Perhaps it came from the need to be with God and yet remain mortal. Prebble was unsure at to its cause but he had read about crazy priests, ranters, perverts, and it was a duty thrust upon him to protect this church, this parish from any such derangements. Not that the present rector was likely to go off his rocker, not that Lucian Fairbrother was likely to rail and rise up. Too long in the tooth, too traditional altogether.

—

5

Lucian went to his G.P. for a check up. Declared fit as a fiddle he then spent some time reading up on miraculous escapes. Babies bounced. Extremely fit service men bounced. Apart from escapologists, stunt men, daredevils who overstepped the mark it appeared that the majority of survivors were ordinary people who fell, landed, flopped against all the odds. There were no sensible explanations. It was seldom to do with prayers, beliefs, the occult. Lucian read the headlines in Exeter library, stared at the faces of smiling, grinning, pleased to be alive folk who had bounced into history for twenty-four hours of fame. There were Americans and Australians and it appeared rather a strong representation from Ireland. A few thanked God. Some had been drunk. Several claimed it was in the family.

Lucian also made visits to the tree. It was actually higher than he had thought. He must have been mad to go up and even crazier to attempt the descent. But plainly there were no large limbs to break his fall. The ground was consistently hard, perfectly ordinary. He should have been killed or at least the subject of multiple major injuries. It was uncanny to be so certain that this should have been the place of his death.

Each time Lucian visited the spot he wondered whether he should fall to his knees and offer an enchanted prayer, or question out loud his maker. He even considered climbing the tree again, re-enacting the whole thing. But where was the point? Whether he lived or survived a second time would not in fact reveal anything about the first fall. And if he did fall again and again and again what was the point of that?

If he accepted his survival as a fact, what he now needed to do was examine not the how but the why. Surely that was it. Was it God telling him something? Or was the trick that he Lucian would now attribute this incorrectly to divine intervention?

He would like to have told Paula. He would like to have gone to his G.P. again and no doubt puzzled and annoyed the man by demanding an X-ray, a complete physical rather than a once-over, the works. He would have liked to discuss the fall from the tree with Sidney.

Alone in the church, afternoon light gently dancing, smell of dying flowers and respectable stench of ancient wood, he had wanted to get this straight with God. Some sort of order, some sort of sense. Did he now, this late in life, have a new job to do? Could there be some purpose, some signal? It didn't have to be dramatic, newsworthy, eye or mind catching. Perhaps the right word in the mind of the dying, or a gesture of kindness to some soul, or a warning (which he had never been good at). Perhaps just the right idea at the right time? He must anticipate it, look out for it, be alert, search. Perhaps, most difficult of all, he must forgive someone.

Richard, Paula, the terrible man Prebble? Who was to be forgiven? Or did it all go back, return to Sidney? For a few seconds the pain beat through Lucian's breast again, the hot tide of guilt and agony, before it left him drenched with sweat and remorse and terrible self-pity. Perhaps I have to forgive myself, he thought.

The light again played across the brass communion rails, it played its variations on the stained glass, it swayed and for a moment or two Lucian felt lifted out of his mortal body, about to float up.

Then the church door noisily opened. Footfalls coming towards him. Lucian kept his back to the man. stayed as if still praying at the pew beneath the pulpit. It was Prebble, he knew... he could smell him.

"Day to you, Rector. Didn't see you there at first. Not used to too many people praying here in the week. Sorry if I disturbed you. Don't want to hurry anybody who's praying."

"Ah yes; yes Prebble. Nice to see you. Well, even the rector has to pray by himself sometimes."

'Rector Clifton used to do it. Each morning; five to ten. Used to come in every week day and read the Collect for the day. Just the Collect. Then he'd say a prayer for anybody who was sick. Used to say it was his job to be here on behalf of those who had to be elsewhere. Everyday he did the same. Not been done since his time of course."

Always polite always low-toned, always measured; Prebble was almost impudent but not quite, always offensive but never over the top, always taking the lead and wrong-stepping Lucian but never foolhardy enough to make an actual statement. He could even understate an " Amen'' Lucian thought. At funerals there was an 'I told you so' tone to his shuffling, his instructing of the men who came to heave the earth over. At weddings there was a 'young will be young ' tone to the way he saw off the bell ringers. At christenings he loudly chimed in the 'Amens' in a totally unnecessary manner. At Friday night choir practices it was a meaningful cough that beat the clock, warning the organist and choirmaster that time was up. He never lied, never exaggerated, never swore, never complained outright. He carried out his work, did it well, did it on time, but somehow he never gave.

'What is it about this place that you love the most?' Lucian asked, getting up from his knees. "For me it's this light, quite unlike anything else" He realised that he'd asked a direct question of Prebble and that he'd probably never done so before. Had he possibly wrong-footed the man?

"This is God's house, not just a place. It's actually His house. Therefore it's my duty to respect it all. We're all visitors here you know., visitors."

Such a knowing statement. Such certainty. Lucian knew again that there was nothing he could do to throw the man, to get to some inner, softer person. The very way he said it inferred that a rector should know better than ask such questions. It inferred that Lucian also was very much a visitor. It inferred that a line of predecessors and probably successors wouldn't dally with such questions. And just to add that pinch of salt Prebble was handing Lucian the highly decorated kneeler for the rector to rehang on its neat little brass hook. It would look untidy unless it were hung up. It would disturb the pew, the line of similar hanging kneelers. It would look as if the rector didn't care.

Lucian, not to be totally beaten, spent some time at his desk in the vestry. Prebble was to be heard pottering about, deliberately noisy.

Lucian looked through a register, fiddled with the time, regretted this obstinacy. A total waste of his time, his intellect, his whittled-down skills. At his age any such loss was to be regretted.

Outside, half an hour later, walking back to the rectory, slow, unsure, his mind went over and over the worry, the tension in his soul, the fall.

Lucian would like to have told Paula about his fall; to create a fresh line of communication with her, to recreate their faith, to share the doubt and possibility of belief.

Lucian would like to have told Prebble about the tree, the climb, the fall, the amazing survival; to shock Prebble, to shake him, to ruin his 'tut tut', his staleness, his assurance, his judgement.

Lucian would like to have spoken to Sidney, or to have dreamed of a conversation with Sidney in the way he used to dream. Perhaps during a walk on the moor, or on a train journey, or even flying to Paris or Cologne or wherever such clarifications could/ might/did take place revealing what we would be, would see, would seem. Or could he turn it back and converse with ghosts; discuss this with his father (the future and the past rattling together in the one dream wind)? Could he reach past this present to let his mother know how he had fallen so?

Lucian would have liked to write this down in a diary, some sort of text. a letter to himself, a secret sermon, a precis or short descriptive bit to be filed away in some mental drawer. But he didn't do such things; it wasn't his style. It wasn't him. So, finally, he had himself to speak to, to bore to death, bash at, as always. "Are you listening to me speaking to you, Lucian? This is me to you, me to me, one to one. This is direct, naked, total, undiluted, self to self. There is no analyst's chair, no passive page, no middle agent, no pulpit here. There may not even be a God here, in it, involved, observing, let alone in control. Let's not kid ourselves that this really was a miracle. Let's try to be smarter than that! For Lucian's sake let's be clear about that!"

But he could not be clear. Running through the mental litter, trying over and over to get to the truth, Lucian (in the garden, in the bath, in the empty church, on the moors, by the river, in Exeter, in the village shops, in his study, in front of the television) could not get nearer it. He began mentally climbing the tree again each night before sleep somehow came. He smelt the grass again, the bark, the lichen, the green of it, the planks at the top. He even sensed the boy down, down below in the game, in the hunting, obeying the rules of the game and the things they did. The game cancelled out the ordinary the dull, the expected, even the real. So hiding there in that tall tree wasn't real? Ah, but it was. The game is a game is a game but it's still real, a changed reality but a reality. He felt the sensation again, what it was like up there looking down, down, down. Another world? No; another view, another way of seeing and being, No more than that. And then the fall, again and again the fall, repeated in his mind (in colour, in red, in white, in grey; in sound, in silence; in huge lumbering shades of sequence). And each night he knew he should have died, should have broken open, should have suffered massive internal damage. But not a thing. None of these things. All of it lost and not relevant and no part of his game, the love of the game, the reality of the existence of the game. 'Oh look at me, I fall and defy all known laws because this is the nature of the game. And I do not need a God to do this. I do not call this a miracle. It simply happens. No God. No witnesses. Nobody to tell of it or to tell it to. Therefore, Lucian old fellow, it cannot exist."

Was it so easy? Was it to be left unsaid? Was he content to let it become a dream, a catch, a something or other never to be defined? A sort of snag in one's spiritual existence? One of the great unexplained? What he used at theological college to call 'the mysties'? Was it for this he toiled at and tried at and attempted faith? The mystery is the mystery itself and not the revelation?

And one day Lucian accepted it as such; mystery, miracle, muddle, mishmash, what did it matter? And another day he yearned to get it straight. And another day it was holy, wonderful, something to be wondered at that God had given him a mental challenge; a sprinkler had been set off above the bald patch of his brain! And another day he was confused. And another day Crusoe-like he set out his pros and cons.

And on the side of miracles there was much fun to be had! A sign, a signal, a new beginning. God's finger poking him into life. Some new work ahead. "Wake up Lucian and get your act together. You thought you were done for, sent out to graze, but it's up and about for you now. Sit up, stand up, get out and see what's ahead. There is unfinished work here. It was for this I saved you from death. You are Lazarus come back with a mission. You are my angel. You are to do this and that. You are to await my sign."

But this was hard. This was a test. This is what he dared not believe but wanted to. This thrust at his humility. This drove him to his knees, to mental sweat, to boil and thrash in his brain. This tested him terribly. This drove him to tears, to actually cry in his bed at night. This made him long, long to tell Paula. But in God's name how to, how to begin?

6

'History' for Peggy Newson was what things became; if it wasn't fact it was the fashion of these fictions that changed and changed. This village was the reason behind so much being venerated and protected in addition to the agricultural wealth. It was the ideas issued between wars and laws and lords and lawyers. It was images of water that flowed between the stones, the landowners, the kings and queens. Living in the village was occupying and being preoccupied by the huge and decorated game of codes and constitutions and conceits. It was a matter of both belief and screaming doubt.

When she saw the old war flags hanging in the church she felt horror. When she saw the precise layout of the fields from the top road leading down to the village, it was for her like observing a peopled map. She could almost inhale the workings of hundreds of years; the messages and meanings were everywhere. But she doubted that many people were in any sense aware of what they were living within.

She was advantaged. She had no farm to tend, no family to take her days; there was no crisis in her life preventing her from expressing her days as she wished. She never felt guilty about this but it did limit her communication. She was terrified that she might bore people. She was afraid that some of her ideas might border on the occult. What was she to tell people about such experiences? And what people?

How could she explain to a gathering of friends, or members of an association, that standing in a manor house she had actually seen other people, seated at boards laid on trestles, or tell them that when visiting an old farmhouse she had seen other cattle and sheep, smaller and thinner, and that several times when looking down onto the village she had seen ploughs drawn by yoked oxen and, once only, she had seen many women cutting grass by hand?

Talking and writing about the manors, the 'hayes', the 'bartons', the origins of parishes, pilgrims, fairs and markets was not the problem. To have seen people passing by in medieval dress, to have smelt the shipping post on a fine, clear day; this was her extraordinary problem. How did one begin to talk about it, particularly if one did not want it to cease?

Once in the churchyard she heard men's voices and women booing. There was nobody at all there. She waited and then saw a woman clad in a white sheet, her hair hanging down, being dragged by some men. They whipped her until she screamed out her admission of immorality. But it was a fine day, with an aeroplane passing overhead and somebody had a transistor radio blaring from one of the small, modern houses nearby. It was both worlds at once.

She wondered if it was the terrible hardships, the flogging and tests of faith that somehow got stuck, coming back for her eyes and mind all these centuries later. Is that why there were no smiling ghosts? Is this why she saw men whom she recognised as Irish paupers, and vagrants and vagabonds, maimed soldiers and seamen, and once at a fair a freak? Were these images caught still by the pain and rage and lack of forgiveness, lack of burial and peace? Didn't this still somehow linger with the country people's distrust of gypsies, an amazing fear still here? How incredible that there were so many variant spellings (as if the evil spell-bound thing could not be captured in a single form): Gipsy. Gippsis, Gipes, Gepsies, Gipsees, Geipseys, Gippseys, Guipsee, Gipses, Gipeseses, Gipsyes, Gpseysà, concerning Outlandish People calling themselves Egyptians, using no craft for merchandise, but deceiving people that they by Palmistry can tell men's fortunes, and so cheat people of their money, and commit many heinous felonies and rotteries...

Gerry Walters, one of the oldest residents who had lived all of his life in the village, knew the gardens and some of the farms and some of the stories of the village. He read nothing about this; it was there about him. The only activity that might have gripped him to the soul of the village in a deeper way, other than spending so many hours in the pubs, was his regular bell ringing. There were six bells, three bearing dates 1637, 1664 and 1705. They had been rehung at the start of this century and although few of the ringers rang and then stayed for the service, the ringing was popular and there were young village lads queuing to take on an older man's place. In some cases this was the main reason for the older men to keep turning up. Once you missed a few Sundays you were likely not to get back in.

These bells, now restricted to Sundays and marriages and funeral tolls, had in years past peeled out to call the devout to services but also to proclaim victories, births or the success of a parliamentary candidate. When royalty or a bishop passed nearby the bells would also proclaim. They might also warn of fires or floods and even announce a local meet of the hounds.

Gerry Walters sensed something of this, but he knew that these huge instruments of sound had also been used to disperse tempests and that there was an older idea of ringing after a baptism to drive the devil away from the sacred waters. If need be he could have decoded 'The Passing Bell,'. The bell age of the deceased would be rung out after the bell had tolled for half an hour, and to announce the sex of the deceased (three times three for a man, three times two for a woman, three times one for a child). Gerry Walters also knew about the bell that had collapsed and killed the oldest clergyman of them all. It was said he had drunk a bit too much and was attempting to ring a curfew, daft old fool.

Miss Bowden the schoolmistress could give the children in her care the colours of history, the bright banners and robes, the ceremonies. She knew about Devonshire folk-songs and cider presses, the turnpikes and highways, the Quakers and militiamen, the coaching days and burials of the dead. She could pass this on and see some of it catch in a child's open mind. But what it meant, what its real power was, this she was less sure about. She was no innovator but as the years passed by she came back on herself, saw herself teaching in the same room, children looking much the same. It was as if she were passing back in time simply because these children raced forward into days of sun and certainty.

One afternoon a ten year old boy had brought in a magazine article about bull-baiting. He had got it from Peggy Newson he said. Miss Bowden didn't read it aloud to the children; there was so much she didn't feel was suitable for their age, but it was another sharp reminder of what history might mean:

..... often the maddened bull would snap the rope that bound it to a stake in the bull-ring and, to the terror of the shrieking people, would charge from one end of the town to the other followed by a mob of bullbaiters, butchers, boys and dogs. A number of these ' bulldogs' were specially bred and trained and heavy wagers were placed on their endurance. Inside the ring of excited men and women, and children as well, holding their dogs, yet more excited, the bull, bound by a rope fastened around the base of its horns or to a collar around its neck, would watch its enemies, vainly testing its strength. Then one of the bulldogs would be let loose and might get tossed by the bull to a height of twenty feet, the crowd rushing forward to catch it and break its fall, for which purposes the women provided themselves with the stoutest of aprons! In doing so the bull might toss or gore a human being, until another dog was let loose and set upon it. Finally the rope would snap and, maddened by pain and fury and set upon by all the dogs, the bull would charge down the main street until at last it was 'ham-strung'. The back tendons of its legs would be cut. Indeed, one of the declared objects of bull-baiting was to make its flesh tender for humans to eat!!

Although Miss Bowden could not bring herself to divulge the terrible truths behind flogging and plagues of witchcraft, she did occasionally manage to send a signal out proving that history and myth and this day and age are bound together in the most curious ways.

The school children, so many coming from farms and cottages, were naturally interested in pets. She thus told them about the place of dogs in history and divulged the history of the dog whipper in particular. She read to them a 1757 Vestry Minute that mixed distemper, madness and muzzling in one entry. It teemed with other messages and histories she dared not relate, but she found herself using this new material (this old extract) as if as a warning to herself, her bumping into herself, her growing old too fast.

Whereas on the 25th day of November last, publick Notice was given in this Town that several Dogs therein had lately run mad, and had bit several other Dogs, who as it was reasonable to apprehend would probably soon be seized with the same distemper, all persons were desired to tie up and confine or muzzle their Dogs for the space of one Month, and during that time proper persons would be appointed to go up and down the Several Streets within the said Town, in order to destroy all such unmuzzled, it being judged as most necessary and the only effective method to put a stop to the progress of so terrible a Disaster...

Peggy Newson remembered at times an introductory sentence to an article about Dartmoor from ' Report and Transactions of the Devonshire Association'. The first sentence read 'The material for this paper is flotsam cast up by the European War. The demand for waste paper has led to the turning out of all manner of old and once valued stores'.

Flotsam... floating wreckage. History is only that part which is finally flung ashore and discovered. It is the discovered part. But then the vast majority of it is left to change, or to totally disappear.

7

Paula hadn't given up, loved Lucian but had now let go. She settled for less and less. It was an act of cowardice and yet confidence, of compassion and yet also a fatal conceit.

For years she had let Lucian empty her, the village employ her, the villagers hire her skills, her time, her talents. But not her own skill, time and talent; only what they assumed she could give, what they felt comfortable with. To be there in church, always, with and without the boys, twice on Sunday. When the organist was ill playing the organ. Attending the Young Wives and running the Mothers' Union. Always there at working parties sales, fêtes, whist drives, those terrible dramatics and concerts and primary school productions.

Her garden was always their garden, her house a place that the villagers could claim, her husband in a special position that offered few advantages. It was assumed she believed in their God, her husband's God, the orthodox God. It was assumed she wanted to arrange church flowers, prepare for the communion, dressing as was expected and smiling on all occasions as if she somehow was beyond personal grief. uncertainty, bare despair.

What did she like to read? Nobody asked her. What music did she really like? Nobody considered. What did she do when alone, Lucian out visiting in the village? Was she ever really alone? Did she ever feel like taking up the telephone and ripping out the cord? Did she ever want to scream out "listen to me, to me". Did she ever want Lucian for herself, to be alone with, as comforter, friend, lover? Did anybody ever think of her as a woman?

Now alone in the house, the telephone off the hook, she waited for Lucian. The Mathews twins were desperately sick and unlikely to live long. Lucian would have to go to the cottage and do his thing; work with his promises and shards of light and special words. They would want that. They would expect that.

And she would behave as if it never touched her, never brought back the memories. She would once he was out resist the appalling urge to read Sidney's letters. To open the suitcase. To take out the letters she had told Lucian she had long ago destroyed. To see the boy's writing from boarding school and then, and then the postcards from all over England when he and Toby were on the run.

She heard Lucian in the porch. She ran to him. "I've just heard from Brian Mathews. The twins aren't going to make it. Can you go over now?"
"Of course, of course; how long ago did they phone? Is Doctor Little there? Can I go dressed like this?"

And he was off in his old jacket, already assuming the role, already the rector on an emergency call and not Lucian her husband, her own, her beloved. Already about his tricks and images and offering something that must truly exist. That is why they wanted him there, to make it real within them.

Lucian walked quickly down the drive and Paula, the phone still off the hook, slowly made her way up to the large rather dark bedroom. He passed by villagers, waved his hand, but stopped for no-one; it would take about three minutes to get there. Why had he not used the car?

Paula sat on the bed. All the letters, the words, the messages were in her wardrobe, in a small suitcase, tied in bundles. Letters from Sidney and from Richard for all their lives. And postcards. And Christmas and birthday cards. Greetings and meanings, regrets and suggestions. Neatly there. Folded over. Perfect in their silence. Some parts of them remembered perfectly before the page was unfolded. A way of leaping time. A way of cheating time.

"I came as soon as I heard," Lucian said, somewhat short of breath.

"Oh do come up; do hurry. They might slip away at any moment. Follow me." An old woman he failed to recognize, not a villager.

Paula now opening the case, sorting out one packet of letters from another, reading the labels. But it was the last ones she wanted. It was always the same; the need, the feel, the recognition, the condition.

She stopped for a moment. Was that a noise downstairs? Was Lucian back? No, he couldn't be. Had he forgotten something? No. Silence. The tick tock of her own obsession.

Lucian's hands shaking the hand of Brian Mathews. Big hands, soiled, now sweaty with fear. He'd cycled back from the tannery. He knew he shouldn't have gone back after lunch.

Lucian's hands moving now to touch, to reach out, to contact Susan Mathews and the twins that she held, in the bed, in the small territory of her protection, in the seconds that were slipping away, in the last lunges of love. The bedroom so small, the light through the small cottage window somehow immense, glowing. The old woman with them there in the room; the room like a cradle.

And Lucian's voice now creating other presences in that room, creating other light and life force, to take away the trouble, the trial, to teach to cope, to educate reason, to touch them all with God's strange purpose. "We pray within our love of these two children, Ruth and Sara, that if you should grant it now their lives should be spared. We beseech you at this time to consider our need for these two babies who have shared this world with us. Give us all strength and a sense of purpose and knowledge of your divine plan, your Almighty purpose. We beseech you to guide us all ....."

Each letter folded, numbered, filed in place within each bundle. She knew the music, the pace, the noises of each one. "Please don't be furious with us. We're quite safe. We'll give ourselves up soon. We just need an adventure. Don't worry about us. We've got money and food and spare clothes. We planned all this ages ago. Please don't inform the police. We know what we're doing. We're totally safe."

Memory like lights dancing, shades, on and off and whistling. Paula could feel the tensions, hear the voices of teachers over the 'phone, see the stern expressions of the police inspector, hear her own doubt. It had gone on and on. Purposeless visits to the school as if there were clues. Interviews with other pupils in the housemaster's and the headmaster's study. Why had Richard heard nothing of the plans, the meticulous preparations? And why had they run away? What on earth did they mean by "needing an adventure'? Who was this boy he'd run off with and why had they not heard anything about him before? No mention. No hints.

Paula recalled the nights lying awake (where were they sleeping?) and rushing to the phone when it rang (more parish calls) and dreading the moment when the newspapers got hold of the story (Rector's Son Missing – Private School Scandal – The 2 Who Got Away). And questions, questions; where did they sleep (hedges, garden sheds, railway stations, bus shelters) and who might discover them (parents, mad old men) and how did they get to so many places (Manchester, Leeds, Sheffield) and who gave them lifts (lorries, trains, private cars) and behind the postcards (so positive, so controlled) what was really going on? And for how long? When would the adventure, stale, go wrong, run into trouble?

Lucian in the small room with the enormous promise of God, the babies now dead, Dr. Little revealing the medical fact. The strong, formal politeness of Brian Mathews. The old woman in tears. And the mother in the bed, herself ill, weak, needing to grip onto something (from Lucian, from the doctor, from her husband) or needing to create rage, a flag of anger to wave in their faces, a noisy banner against reality and God and the awful truth. Lucian leaving now, leaving his words in the room, beside the hurt. Walking back, waving again at villagers who passed, hearing the church clock strike the hour. New time beginning.

Each card with its picture of a different place with almost the same message. Had she prayed? Did she now remember how? Was it to protect, to direct, to purchase some sense of hope; to keep it a safe adventure'? Or was it praying against: perverts, molesters, murderers, oddballs, or perhaps something more ordinary like catching a cold, an accident of some sort, something that treated in time and properly could be corrected, cured?

She heard Lucian at the front door. She heard him enter, heading for the security of his study. Surrounded by books, puffing at his pipe, he would sit there waiting for her to make some tea. He wouldn't come upstairs. He wouldn't seek her. There was no need to hurry to hide away the letters. She wouldn't have to pretend to have been tidying up the bedroom. She wouldn't have to bother with any of that.

"The twins have died,' Lucian said. "They slipped away whilst I was there. I couldn't do anything at all. I was as usual left with gestures and words."

Paula, pouring tea, listened to his account of the visit. She couldn't really see it, the room like a cradle, the small room crowded with care that did no good, the special light in the room, the mother in the bed. Years of deaths and comforting words and burials and funerals had reduced her ability to see such scenes. Feeling sad was hopeless, like Lucian's words. Even the death of babies was something that became part of the job, the calling, the role that Lucian played and nothing startling, nothing to make you rage. Nobody was going to run out onto the lawn and scream at God and shake a fist at the sky. Not even the parents would do that. Paula knew just what the mother would do. A secret place in the heart. A hollow that would remain for ever. A place that no new love or music or roar of success could ever take away.

She could hear Lucian talking. He needed these words. He needed her to listen, or simply to be there... She heard him out of respect, a kindness. a slow compassion.

"If God is a light in the mind, if that's true, then what do we do when that light goes out? What on earth do those two parents do? What terrible distraction could cancel out their grief? Oh yes: time and time and other people's words. But what do they say to themselves?"

Paula knew that Lucian wouldn't take this lightly, wouldn't be able to set it aside as he should have done, as she would. It would prick at his belief, taunt his concept of faith, set up a ripple of challenges.

How old he looked. She could see his father in him. That stern old monster with God thrashing down on life, every day a trial, all existence to be measured and defined. But when he wasn't speaking, preaching, ranting, he was a fine looking man, white hair still thick, a face that might have inspired, the sort of face in an oil painting that would halt you. Lucian as he grew older increasingly ghosted that stern quality, when he was particularly tired or upset or inwardly angry.

Paula hadn't given up, still loved him, still shared some of his purpose and seriousness at times like this. Years ago she would have offered to visit the mother. Not now; she wouldn't offer now. But she took Lucian's hands in hers and stood by his chair in the room as the silence of their own thoughts surrounded them.

8

Mrs Waley lay in her large, damp bedroom at Dean's House; her home for fifty-three years, her small universe, a place she never left now. It was nearly nine a.m. Soon Mrs Pratley would come to knock on her bedroom door with the hot water, and then the breakfast, and then the post (very small these days) and then help her to dress for another day.

The days of carriages and foreign travel and dinner parties and shadowing her husband were over. His study was dusted each week. The visiting sun passed through it and the huge reception rooms and the ornate lounge and formal dining room. The numerous shutters were opened and closed each day. But the rooms gathered silences, no longer conversation, laughter, whispers, the sounds of lives and motions of dreams.

Today the rector would call, at 11 a.m. He would be ushered into Mrs Waley's bedroom by one of the maids, to be seated opposite her high armchair at the far end of the room. Mrs Waley had not been in the garden for six years. She had not left her bedroom suite for three years. She would never venture out again. The Queen Anne mansion would continue to slide into obscurity and destruction until her death and then the college, a mile away, would inherit all of the remaining estate. Dean's College would carry on the place name perhaps for years, The Waley Memorial and Waley Trust and Scholarship Scheme would travel on in time benefiting those as yet unborn.

Mrs Waley lay waiting. She was fully aware of the state of her room, she sensed the gradual decay that must be dragging into every corner of the house. She did not need to inspect the window washes, the roof tiles, the paintwork, the rust and lichen and mapshaped dampness. She knew that the elms in the park had died, the rose garden lay in ruins, the lawns had become bits of pasture that not even the goats could keep down. She knew that Burton and his boy did their best to keep things from total disorder (the central heating system, the guttering, the fences and hedges, the goats, a few chickens) and that Mr Hurst maintained revenue from the farm cottages. She did not need to see, to inspect, to go on grand tours any more. Mr Hurst and Burton and Mrs Pratley and maids she seldom saw (and had never known the names of) kept chaos at bay. And once a year the family solicitor met her for an hour in her bedroom, sat opposite her in this same room, telling her things she didn't really want to know.

She could hear the church clock striking. She received holy communion from the rector once a month in this room. She studied The Times as if news from elsewhere remained part of an essential etiquette along with Dr Maxwell's report on her health (twice a year).She wrote no letters. She no longer listened to the radio. There had never been a television in the house. She kept Elgar and Venice and Athens and her parents in her head. She kept walking in the Malvern Hills and climbing in Zermatt and the gold Italian evenings there. She kept a small island off the Turkish coast there. Each morning fresh flowers came into her room. She did not ask where they came from. What she saw when she looked out from either of the two large windows she never spoke about.

Lucian enjoyed the coffee, the house stuck in old time, the trapped presence of the house, even the echoes in the main hall on arrival.

He always walked to Dean's House; it seemed appropriate using the track that had once been used by house parties and by Mrs Waley and her parents and then by Mrs Waley and her husband, Sunday by Sunday for years and years. It was ill defined now, totally obscured in places and even ploughed over in parts but he was determined to keep to it. Some sense of history, of human record, of refusing to let it go. It was ridiculous he knew but essential to him. Somehow he sensed that he owed the family this respect. The Waleys had supported the church in numerous ways for many years. There were several small trusts benefiting the church and parish each year. Within Mrs Waley's will there was an annual expectation of at least two thousand pounds. Should some major church renovation be required Lucian would have had no hesitation in requesting a substantial additional sum from Mrs Waley.

"There is an item that I wish to talk about, Rector; and I don't think we should wait any longer to set the work in hand. My husband collected numerous items on his travels as you know and all but one have already been sent to museums or mentioned in my will. However, there is one very special item that came into his hands in a most unusual way many years ago and had it not been for Mr Hurst I would surely have forgotten it. It is extremely old and has far longer than I can remember resided in the byre. It is I am afraid pagan and it may not be acceptable to you at all, but I want you to see it and make up your own mind. I have arranged for Burton to show it to you, this morning."

Lucian had to wait for Burton to arrive. Standing at the ,front of the house he could see the church far off and the trees surrounding the rectory, and in the opposite direction the buildings of Dean's College.

His mind was already racing. What did he expect? Some small fertility symbol? Some ancient sculpture in wood or stone smuggled here by Mr Waley, and why had it been hidden away in the byre for so long? Why had Mrs Waley over coffee and biscuits been so brief, her normal manner somehow limited, her small attempts at humour and anecdotes kept at bay?

She certainly knew her subject, she wasn't likely to confuse some relic with something of real power. What did she anticipate that might surprise him? The church had its measure of pagan symbols in pew carvings, certain creatures and signs that few of the congregation had deciphered, in wood and stone and in one small window in stained glass. Certainly there were a few of the faithful who knew of the primary pagan customs that lay behind well-dressing and rush-bearing and other ceremonies of garlanding, celebrating and protecting. They were aware that at Christmas and Easter old gods had been accommodated, baptised anew, that the blood of ancient things was still flowing. Lucian had himself attempted to keep some associations alive on Plough Sunday. He had never banned the use of mistletoe at Christmas. He had even blessed fields and tractors and barns. In his own mind he knew where hope for the present and fears of the future mingled in the minds of ordinary people who nevertheless could not easily speak of fundamental fertility, the ache of ancient blood, the demands of flesh to create more fundamental connections. They required decent deities, clean and in bright raiments, the ancient roar and rage and pain was best left obscure in poetic texts.

Lucian recalled troubles in other parishes when certain objects had been discovered as pagan. Some had been removed or changed or obscured. In his own parish there had been a major row about gravestones. It had been suggested in the diocese that in order to make the churchyard upkeep easier the ancient stones should be moved and placed beside the churchyard walls or the church itself. The churchyard might then become a place of well kept lawns and flower beds. Only the graves of those long gone would be moved.

The resulting dissent was decent, orderly, well voiced, yet beneath it lay an ancient superstition that no logic could appease. It would take years of cremations and a new generation of faithful churchgoers to correct. Was this particularly significant in the villages? Would the closure of town churches and the desecration of holy places (making way for new roads and car parks and shopping centres) gradually lead the way or was the village church and churchyard a place of more significant sensitivity? Did these ancient stones of church and burial epitaph contain actual souls; had they indeed come to be God's own things? Was the fight in stained glass God's holy light rather than a glorious symbol of his light? Were some of these old things never to be put away? Did people still perceive the moon in the ancient Celtic cross? Was a holy well made holy by men or by God? Was the earth mother and the god of pasture still present behind the symbols and ceremonies, the Christian dictum merely a comforting cloak changing the face but not the fact of the faith?

In the byre Burton, unsure of himself and certainly of Lucian, began to clear a pathway through crates, garden wrought iron furniture, rolls of pig wire, old hen houses, debris, bean poles, remnants of garden fêtes, archery targets, debris, debris, debris.

"Can't hardly get anywhere in here any more. Needs a lot of sorting out and burning."

"Perhaps I can help?" suggested Lucian, sensing the man's coldness.

"Oh no; not suitable work for you sir; you stay there till I can make a way through."

Burton didn't attend church. Once, Lucian thought, he was a bell ringer but not now. One of those faces he met in the village, at the fête; one day a face to meet at a funeral, a burial, ready to share his grief, ready for some sense of God then.

"I ought to get in here one day and sort the lot out. Just look at it! Been like this for years, Lord knows how long. Bits of a car in here somewhere, under all this. Used to be kept regular, each thing in its proper place. See these packing cases; I've orders to keep them here till she dies. Lord knows what's in them. Quite valuable I'm told."

Dust, dirt, debris; Waley treasures ready to go to museums and now the parts of a Daimler and now more pig wire and empty wooden barrels.

"Man came here about a year ago and wanted to buy all the old farm stuff. Wheels and gardening implements and stuff we used to use at hay making. Said they were all of value. Offered to take them all. Trouble is now he knows they're here. That's why I keep it all locked up."

The work continued and Lucian felt even more useless. Why wouldn't the man let him assist. Was it some sense of order or didn't Burton trust him? Probably the former. And did he know what he was looking for?

"Where is it, exactly?" Lucian asked.

"At the back, right at the back. Nobody can see it there. Don't know why it ever came here. If you don't mind my saying so, sir, I don't rightly see why you're interested in it. Piece of filth it is. Piece of dirty old porn. 'Spect you'll think the same when you see it. Ah; here it is. Under this sheet, hidden away from view thank God. Here she is.'

Burton backed away from whatever it was. He came back to where Lucian was waiting.

"Now it's ready for you sir. I'll not stay here till you've finished. I'll come back in a few minutes if that's all right. I don't expect it will take more than that. That's long enough for her."

He walked off leaving Lucian all the more amazed. Was Burton being specifically rude or was there something he really disliked back there in the byre? Dirty old porn? Was it a relic from Pompeii perhaps or from India? Some phallic sculpture or mosaic and why did Mrs Waley want him to inspect it? For what purpose?

Lucian made his way to the rear of the byre. It was light enough to see. A stone figure designed to fit in a wall, about eighteen inches tall, the face round and grinning, the legs wide apart, a grinning figure with knees wide apart, a woman figure with fat hands gripping open the lips of her vulva, her genital gesture totally unambiguous; a sheela-na-gig grinning at Lucian through the light and time and meanings of centuries.

9

The Mathews twins were to be buried rather than cremated. A small grave for two brief lives.What was the point of it?

Lucian, composing himself to write another sermon, reflecting on his fall, the deaths of the twins, May Day, the strange bequest of Mrs Waley; contemplating his own feelings as much of those of the congregation that might listen to him. What did they expect? Confirmations, challenges, the light of adoration rather than inquisitions, God's great 'yes', rather than his 'perhaps'. Indeed, did they need the sermons at all, to mean anything more than being there in a church on a Sunday between prayers and psalms and hymns, the architecture of God on earth. Were Prebble's assertions commonly held?

Did the farmers need Lucian to reflect upon nature for them? Did the women need a priest to define God's purpose in the deaths of babies? Sometimes Lucian began to favour the Quaker silences, the pause for other voices to speak, the ability to. Let silence cleanse the mind and soul, the rejection of priests naming the nameless and finding words for things beyond human description.

What would he say as he buried the twins, and would he between the set texts find his own words, his own place? Was he still capable of true and convincing originality?

In a nearby village another clergyman had attempted an original voice. a bold concept, a glorious image. Inspired by the need to inspire, to get past the orthodoxy, to breathe new life, he had begun to remove the church pews to permit drama and song and even dancing as part of the essential celebration of his church services. The row this provoked had split the village and Lucian had for some reason been invited to accompany the archdeacon at a special church meeting.

Lucian vividly recalled the hall packed with agitated and curious parishioners, many of whom had not set foot in the church for years.The scandal had been fanned by the local Press, fed by informants who disliked the vicar's revolutionary ideas or his young wife or any idea of change. The vicar's warden and the people's warden took opposing sides. The headmistress of the local primary school and the organist sided with the vicar whilst the local vet and two doctors and a Colonel Hewett fiercely defended the pews, the status quo, the place of hymns and words. Dancing in church and recitation were the devil's things along with drama and guitar accompaniments. The vicar should have known better. Surely he was too old to be trendy? What on earth had got into the man? He had to be stopped.

The heat in the crowded hall had been immense, Lucian recalled. He remembered the look of intense animosity on the faces of some of the men. He recalled the archdeacon's struggle to create order, to chair any sort of a discussion. He had begun by trying to establish some facts. He had perhaps unwisely attempted to lecture them.

"Before you leap to accuse your vicar of ultra modern ideas, I would beg you to consider two things; a church is fundamentally a collection of people united in worship. It is not in this respect a place, a building, bricks and mortar. And then a second point; it is to be used as that collection of people desires. Should they wish to change the furnishing, change this or that, and equally extend their form of worship, there are no fundamental objections to this. It is not morally or theologically wrong."

There were cries of protest from some of those assembled, even cries of "blasphemy" and "the church is not a dance hall" before the man could continue.

"Ah yes: to dance. To sing. To worship God with such artistic gifts! All very ancient practices I assure you, all much beloved by the ancient worshippers…"

"And by the terrible prostitutes," called out one of the younger farmers.

The archdeacon was not to be put off, if anything he gathered strength.

"Let me try to help you. If we are to resolve this matter we must get one thing clear. Are you objecting to the idea of change itself or to the nature of the change?"

This was not understood, so the archdeacon attempted to clarify. "Are you actually against the removal of the pews or annoyed because you feel this change is being imposed? You must make this clear to me and to yourselves."

A few people then spoke out. One well-spoken man protested at the destruction of ancient carvings. He was told that no actual destruction was intended; the pews would be carefully removed to the side aisle and could be replaced. Only a few of them would be removed in fact.

The people's warden did his best to fairly represent the views of the dissenters. They had not been fully consulted and yes they did object to the very nature of the change. The pews were a fundamental part of worshipping. The archdeacon corrected this belief, pointing out that pews had only been introduced to the church some considerable time after it had been built and used for worship. "You know, this was so of many old churches; there were no pews. The congregation stood, moved about, were somewhat noisy and generally stank! If you wanted a seat you had to bring it with you. In Crowland Abbey there is a stone bench running round the wall for the old and infirm. Hence the saying "The weakest go to the wall." You know even Pepys makes reference to this; he wrote of parishioners having to build their own pews, hence pew rents. I believe I am correct in saying that this church was not properly fitted out with pews until 1746. Is that not so vicar?"

It was then made quite clear that animosity towards the vicar and his wife ruled the emotions of those assembled in the hot little hall. They disliked his wife, his evident learning, his interest in cultural things. He was a changer, a bringer-in of new things. The row about pews wasn't about pews but about personalities and politics. This was quite clear in the archdeacon's mind.

Perhaps the archdeacon had invited Lucian to witness this in order to deter him from similar small revolutions. Had the man perhaps sensed some restlessness in Lucian's work or manner of speech suggesting a rebellion to come? Probably there had been no more than a need of a supporter in case things had got out of hand.

Now, in his study, Lucian reflected on his predicament and the position of his own parishioners. There were men who farmed all week and who came to church near exhaustion most Sundays. There were men who came to ring the church bells but who never stayed to worship. There were men who stripped skin from pigs and slit the throats of sheep, who picked up rats in their hands to kill them and who entered the church as the meekest of creatures, capable of tears at festivals and on Remembrance Sunday. On Sundays these men and their wives mixed with teachers and doctors and solicitors, people who virtually inhabited different planets, all made one at the communion rail. What force was this? What sense of wonder? Could they all receive Lucian's sermon in the same way? Did they achieve their own meanings? And did the wives of such different men make meanings again, gather up solaces, find their own poetry and truths in the same prayers and hymns?

And here, in this same church, summoned by the same bells, these people sit down in pews and stand up to sing with ghosts. Not the revenging, lonely, hurt souls but the spirits created in this place; the same sounds and words and texts going out and out, echoing, repeating. Thus the young man repeats what his grandfather repeated in his day, in his way, in his little history.

Lucian once again considered the sermon, its form, its place in the procession of things, the order of expectations and how truth and the new came often from reinforcements, repetition rather than resolution.

And then it struck him. Of his entire congregation it was Paula who stood out, who more than any other person probably rejected this. She clung to certain things in herself, rarely shared, seemed less and less capable of holding out her hands to him in love, in peace. The sorrow in her grew and grew and gathered no cloak of understanding. It was as if Sidney were running away to die each day.

10

How to bury, to cloak in words and prayers, to lower gently or consume in flames, to scatter, the garlands of grief gently soaking in rain, in dew, in natural decay?

Standing at the graveside now, two small coffins to be lowered into this gentle space, this resting place, this strange abode of earth and silence and natural decay. The voices to say farewell, the hymns to say farewell, the faces to say it, the tears to mean it; the loss between the grief and groping for hoping, new life, eternity, continuation. Two coffins, two babies; the words hopeless and yet essential, Lucian doing his job so well and yet equally numbed, confounded, digging deep into his own spiritual reserve.

This year alone he had prayed at the burial of Simon Roberts (mentally limited since birth, a burden to his mother, an embarrassment to his brother, a sign of failure to his father), and old Annie Pratt (small, frail, faithful servant who had for years hobbled to her pew, to her solace, to her place of peace), and Andrea Prozorsky (Polish, waiting in different parts of England for her husband of one year to join her, to escape, to find her and start the new life) and so many others. How could one small village offer up so many? How could he speak for them all? How could he embrace the meaning of their lives and deaths and do it perfectly, with meaning, with his own-time belief, his own certainty?

And here, in this place of stones and inscriptions, how could he gather up the trust of so many mourners, who needed to know, who needed to feel the love continuing, who needed to make a journey with their loved ones?

Lucian stood over the grave in the place selected by Prebble. The grave gaped as it always did. No amount of prayers and hymns could conceal its fundamental simplicity, its crude shape, its purpose. To put the body down in dark earth, to lower that which is so much loved into silence and earth and decay, to cover it gently with our love and hope and symbols of belief, to cover it with soil and darkness and regret and flowers and small texts. To pause and walk away. To shake hands and assemble in a small abode and repeat the ancient assurances. To walk away. To leave the dead in the place of the dead. To remember what the living was, the life was, to grasp at whatever the small hours and days gave us. But in this case, for these babies, what was the purpose and what was the promise? What was the meaning of such brief blooms? Colonel Noel had died in his arms, in the midst of bedside communion. He had been totally at peace. He had had time to prepare. And for others, a long life well lived, it was the natural order, it was almost rehearsed, it was to be expected and accepted. The pain of departure was no less but it was meaningful, it was something that one could explain.

Lucian, burying the twins with all the certainty he could muster, feared the father's words more than the sobbing of the mother. He felt the rage, the unrelenting anger, the huge threat of disbelief. It challenged his faith, each text, the hymns, the prayers, each element of the ceremony, his own purpose as priest.

What was a man like Brian Mathews meant to do? Where should he take his rage, his impotence, his loss, his fist of fear and self-dread? To scream at God, to break into blasphemy, to hurl his logic at his priest, to bellow and storm at his wife, to reach back seeking a purpose for revenge, judgement, settlement? Did such grief sink deep into his bones and soul breeding a silence, a certainty of defeat, a grand disdain and doom? Or did he chew on his pain, grasp for the love of his wife, make promises for the future, determine to be a better husband, try to thank God as the thought of a future roared before him? Lucian dreaded the man's eyes, the man's silence, the way Brian Mathews kept his head down as he sat with his wife in their cottage and cups of tea and plates of sandwiches were passed round. A small, simple family now gathered in, tight, in harmony, in awkward peace, in the silence of disbelief,The future like some dreadful wilderness, the normal facts and functions appearing ludicrous, even the sound of their clock in the living room, even the telephone ringing, even the little envelope carrying details of a Death Grant. Even the light in Brian Mathews' garden; another light now, a different place, almost an ancient place, the sweat on Brian's hands like dirt, like grease, like something he couldn't get clean. The silence in that small bedroom total, physical. And in the small room opposite, with the two cots, the light quite white, the colour of silence, of some ancient and terrible decision.

Lucian, returning to the church, saw Prebble at the graveside, presumably checking that all was in order. What did a man like Prebble make of this? And later Lucian went to stand by the blooms and brief handwritten messages to pray, to pause, to attempt something beyond words.

For hundreds of years these funeral processions had come here and the bodies had begun their decay. There had been other babies and soldiers and other cut down lives. There had been scenes of huge grief and anger. People had screamed their rage. Men had yelped like young boys. Women had placed small scenes and the noises of conversations deep in the secret places of their hearts. The living had slipped a little nearer their own deaths each time.

Lucian stood with nobody else present for about half an hour. Images of old people, of his own mother and father, of dead patients at the psychiatric hospital, of soldiers in the trenches, of a girl sinking in mud on the television news, of a school in Wales, of tiny coffins being stacked in a pit by prisoners in the U.S.A., of babies in Hiroshima, of near to death babies in the arms of beggars in Cairo, images of infant deaths ran quietly through his mind.

Dropping to his knees Lucian tried to make a prayer, to put all this into words of purpose, to defeat the howl of the 'why?' thundering in his head.

He left the grave to its silences. It was to be a fine, clear night. That made it easier. Memories of burials in mid-winter filtered through his memory. Even memories of burials in floods when the coffins almost floated.

Perhaps the parents would visit the site before darkness fell. Perhaps he would not be the only one to fall to his knees and consult the soul.

In the early hours it was Prebble who came, but he did not stand to pray or reflect. He came alone with a lamp but he didn't need to light it. The light of moon and stars and a brilliant night sky at one a.m. made it possible for him to get on with his work without the aid of the lamp initially. He dug a shallow grave about twelve yards away from where the wreaths and bunches of flowers lay, silver now in the moonlight. He cut expertly into the turf and stacked the sods neatly. He worked with the briefest of pauses, stopping to wipe the sweat from his forehead. He had brought all the necessary tools in a bundle of sacking. He knew his craft well. The small shallow grave began to take shape. He consulted his watch between the chimes of the church clock. He was in a hurry and he was afraid.

When the new grave was ready Prebble refreshed himself with a bottle of cold tea and began to carefully remove the wreath and flowers, setting them beside the freshly dug grave. He then started on the major task of digging up the freshly thrown-in soil. It was a monstrous task taking all his strength, his stubborn will, his determination. By degrees he slowed down, had to stop to mop his brow more often, had to swig from the bottle.

When another man joined him, coming up out of the dark green light, Prebble hardly paused, evidently expected him.

Now the work gathered speed, the earth heaved up onto a growing pile, the digging in rhythm, the men both determined to get to the two small coffins so recently laid in the silence.

Both men found it difficult to hoist up the coffins. They struggled as if guilt or physical pain or both grabbed at them.

At six a.m. with the sky all the time changing hue, they placed the two coffins in the shallow grave, filled it in, carefully placed the flowers, made it as neat as they could. They then filled in the other grave, and spent a considerable amount of time replacing the sods and making the spot look good. Then, saturated with sweat, both Prebble and his assistant Burton left the graveyard. They walked down the streets looking at their watches and looking out for early risers. A dog barked. From afar they heard a car starting.

At Prebble's cottage the men parted but not before Prebble had gone into his cottage and come out again to pay Burton in cash.

At five-thirty a.m. the graveyard was slowly cloaked in a new light. Then bird chorus, the stones catching shades of gold, the face of the church clock shining, flowers on the fresh grave damp and holding into themselves deep scents, realms of beauty, symbols of passing into new creation.

And then a figure was there in the dawn light, Brian Mathews who had left his cottage and the hollow rooms to be here at the graveside, to be here at the beginning of a new day, to be standing here as if the twins would sense it, welcome it, know of him.

Exhausted by his weeping rage, by his isolation, by all the care he had given his wife and the people who had crowded into his grief, he fell to his knees at the grave, as if he would fall into the thick bank of blooms, the mount of messages on little cards, the symbols from other souls.

11

"Paula, I think we ought to talk; about ourselves."

Paula, gardening, looked up from the flower bed where she crouched. Lucian held out a mug of tea. It was one of those brilliant days when working inside was impossible, when the garden appeared to be actually bulging with intentions, the green fat with purpose, the lawns folding over with energy.

She got up now to join Lucian in one of the old wicker garden seats.

"What a day! What a wonderful day to be alive," said Lucian.

"And so why are we going to risk spoiling it?"

"Spoiling it?"

"By talking about ourselves. What is there to say?"

"I need to share things with you, not simply report on my day, my work. I need to share things and feel that you are by my side."

"As a wife or as a co-worker, the willing right hand woman, the parson's wife as a free of charge worker; which is it to be?" asked Paula with minimum humour.

"As Paula, my wife," replied Lucian. "I need to tell you about ..."

They could hear the telephone ringing. They both waited for it to stop.

"Might be urgent," said Paula.

"Might be," said Lucian, "but then so is this conversation."

The ringing continued.

"Could be another death or Richard or Maureen or-."

"And it's probably the wrong number," said Lucian.

The ringing stopped. Lucian, determined to grasp the moment, was surprised to hear his own voice sounding so urgent, so vehement. "Look, we've got to get a few things said. I feel as if for all our love, all our trust, we are drifting. It's not that I want to burden you with parish chores, God forbid! It's not that I can do anything to change our lives, to make amends, to make up to you the loss of Sidney but -"

"Sidney! Why Sidney, why do you mention his name?"

Lucian looked at Paula, long and hard. "Because, Paula, because his memory has created a wall between us. Your grief never ends, your blame even. You won't let go. You are living half a life. You don't fully live with any of us,

Richard or me or Maureen or Thomas; we all feel you cutting us off. And, Paula, it has to come to an end, my dear, it really has to end."

The silence was interminable. Lucian dreaded what his words might have done. Why had he spoken out now? What was his purpose?

Paula, finally, slowly responded. "You are right, of course. It is half a life, half here and half in the past. All these years part of me has never left the days when Sidney was alive, was here, was part of us. His death has never left me. His going off, running off from school, his adventure. And then his death. I'm not even sure it would not have been better had he simply died earlier or at school or in some other way. At least he would have died as the Sidney we knew. His adventure must have changed him, must have been the result of some change. It means that when he died he wasn't the same boy."

Lucian has not meant to get into this. He had really wanted to talk about his fall from the tree or his feelings at the twins grave or about his visit to Mrs Waley and the sheela-na-gig. He would have liked to tell Paula about his continuing dislike of Prebble, of his feeling that life was possibly about to change, of his need for her, of his need to change the living of their lives. He would like to have told her of his need to scream.

But the moment was going, the telephone was again ringing and Paula was rising to answer it.

"Paula, don't go, don't answer the thing. Let's settle this now. Please, let's not lose the moment."

"No. Lucian; it's no good. It's not your fault, it's mine. I can't give up, I can't change. We will have to make the best we can of half of me."

"It's not fair to any of us and it's not fair to you."

Paula was by now about to enter the house. She turned at the doorway and looked back at Lucian. For a second he thought she would not enter, would leave the phone, would return to him.

"I know," she said, "it's not fair to any of us." Then she went into the house, the old life, the old self, half of her clinging to a dead son who had he lived would have changed, would have left them anyway, might have died some other way.

Lucian sat, alone, aware of his loneliness within the brilliant garden, within his parish, within his being. The life he wished to lead was not possible any more. What he had to do now was not cling to the wreckage but invent, create some bright new thing. An adventure for himself? Is that what Sidney's death was to teach him, all these years later; an adventure? Had falling from a tree and the activities of the last few days and this attempt at touching Paula come down to this? It's later than you think old friend. Get out and make a new wonder, don't wait for it to make you new. The miraculous doesn't happen, it's a matter of a number of sensations or energies finding at one moment a vacuum to fill. It is their independence, their total lack of relationship that creates in a unique moment and action a new thing. Only a divine being can repeat it.

Lucian, knowing that Paula was deep into a telephone conversation with Maureen, called out his love and good wishes and made his way up to the large bedroom.

He found the suitcase easily enough, found inside it as he expected the letters and cards he knew she had not destroyed.

He didn't read one of them. Carefully he took them out and separated those sent by Sidney on his 'adventure'. He still resisted the urge to read them, to interfere with their truths, to let their strange nature sting him again.

The other letters and cards and greetings went back into the suitcase in neat piles. Lucian then carefully collecting all Sidney's messages into his arms made his way downstairs again.

He placed each letter, each card, on the large kitchen table, in neat lines, each envelope almost touching the other, each card edge to edge. The entire table surface was covered.

He heard Paula put the receiver down.

"Paula; I'm in the kitchen. I need to discuss something with you."

She came in and immediately saw the table covered with envelopes and cards. Or did she see secrets, evidence, lies, truths, treasures, things that could not come here, be viewed, be discussed?

The silence as she slowly walked round and round the table was almost unbearable.

Lucian's voice was very gentle. "We can burn them now. You can do it. Burn them now. Or we can bury them. You can do that as well or I can. I can help you. You see we have to do one or other, Paula, we have to do this. We have to finally bury our dead. We must not go on without doing this. We must not give way and lose this moment. We have to act now."

He saw her carefully collecting up the treasures, as if in some set order, as if she could tell a sequence. She didn't look at him until she had finished.

"We will bury them," she said, her voice firm. "We will do what you do with the dead. We will settle them down in the soil. Here, we will use this old biscuit tin, it will become a coffin for words. It will do nicely. You are right; we will do it now. We will settle this finally. I will never mention these letters again."

She lightly kissed his cheek and they went out into the garden and she took up one of her spades and Lucian followed her, amazed by her resolve, to the far left hand corner of the garden. Beneath the Christmas tree that they themselves had planted when Sidney was alive Paula began to dig.

"Not a large hole," she said, "not a large space for a tin of words. Do you remember how the boys used to bury dead birds and dead mice this way, in old tins and boxes?"

"You are very brave my dear," said Lucian finally, "far, far braver than I."

"There; it is done. Nobody will see those words any more. It is quite done."

Her courage deserted her then and so she hurried ahead of Lucian and began to work at the flower bed.

In half an hour her entire life had changed.

12

Prebble stood in the small waiting room with Burton. Both men were extremely nervous.

"Let me do the talking," said Prebble.

"You bet I will," said Burton, "it's all your doing anyway. I only helped with part of it."

"Oh no; that's not true," said Prebble, "you arrived late because you fell asleep otherwise you'd have been there on time and we would have finished earlier and made a better job of it. Anyway, you took your pay in full didn't you?"

The men scowled at one another. Prebble sensed that he had to retain his authority. "You let me sort this out with the rector; I know how to handle him. You just leave it to me."

But he was uncertain, terribly afraid of the consequences. He had to tell the truth, all of it, and somehow get the rector to protect him. He couldn't get the rector in on it so how, how could he get the protection? Could he expose the man, threaten him, challenge him in some way? Would the risk of scandal in the parish be enough? Prebble had found no way through his worry, his muddle, and all the time the threat from Brian Mathews beat on his mind. Mathews had guessed at once, of course, had come straight to Prebble, had threatened to beat him up and expose him and have him dismissed. And so had Fred Summers, in the company of his wife.

Lucian welcomed both men, surprised to meet Burton again, curious to note what a state Prebble was in. Deep inside him that was some sense of satisfaction in seeing Prebble nettled.

"I suggest you tell me the entire story, from the beginning. I need to know every detail and for how long this has been going on. Only then can I work out a course of action. I must warn you also that I cannot guarantee in any way at all not to take these matters further. Now, take your time, we shall not be disturbed."

In the next few minutes Prebble would have been glad of a disturbance, to grasp some thinking time, to consider how the rector was reacting, to see if he had come up with a way through, to save himself and his position. If only he could involve others, if only he could appear not to be the only one, if only the rector were to feel that he must also take some responsibility, if only Burton were to be seen as equally guilty and other assistants before him.

"It began years ago, long before my time," Prebble began. 'There's always been some sort of system, official and unofficial. People have either officially reserved a burial place, for which they have had to pay, or they've come to me or my predecessors."

"Of course they have paid you as well," butted in Lucian.

"Well, yes, of course, but much less than if they'd done it officially. And then with me they have got what they wanted, the precise place in the churchyard, near a favourite tree or with a special view to or from the village or near the beloved ones or things like that. Doing it officially meant you needed money and a good reason and some authority. You needed to be regular churchgoers as well. With me it was plain and simple; pay up and you get your space."

"How much?" asked Lucian.

Prebble shuffled in the chair uneasily. Burton was attentive.

"It depended."

"On what?" asked Lucian. He was determined to prevent Prebble from missing out uncomfortable facts.

"To reserve a grave meant an annual payment of £10. That meant reserving the space on my own little plan. I keep it all in a notebook see. Then I need to make sure it stays reserved and that the official record doesn't spoil my scheme. I need to keep the official record clear of mine. Once or twice there have been near misses but I've always got my way. As I dig the graves I can come up with some pretty convincing reasons against one plot or another. Tree roots making it unsuitable for example or an integral spring or too much clay or rock even. There's always been a reason."

"A set of convincing lies, you mean," said Lucian.

"If it seemed convincing to them there was no harm done," replied Prebble. "It's all worked well enough for years and years. There's really been no harm in it."

"Up to now," said Lucian. "What exactly went wrong?"

"I made a mistake. A long while back. I double booked. I had a space reserved in my book for the Summers family. I'd transferred it from my predecessor's book. I made a mistake then and a mistake when I altered the official record. One said one thing and one another. Fred Summers kept paying me his £10 each year and Mathews began his payments later and all should have been well. Then those twins died and got buried in the Summers' place. They threatened me, to expose me, and later Mathews threatened to beat me up and…"

"I still don't understand what you are saying. How does Brian Mathews come into this?" Lucian asked.

Prebble faltered. The rector hadn't guessed the whole terrible truth.

"We dug up the twins. We dug them up and moved them down a bit into a spare place. Mathews went to visit the grave and saw that we'd moved it. Only a few yards but he noticed it and guessed the reason at once. Now I've got the Summers on one side and Mathews on the other."

"And apart from all the money you've been taking you've actually dug up two babies and deposited them somewhere else!"

"Only a few yards down."

"A few yards down!" exclaimed Lucian, rising from his chair. "A few yards down! And I suppose you used the burial service, you blessed the ground, you made sure God knew. Good heavens man, I'm not sure how many crimes you've committed by your foolish act! It's beyond belief I really hardly credit it!"

"It wasn't just me, Rector; it's been going on for years. It's not fair to blame me alone!" protested Prebble, hoping for support from Burton.

But Burton was silent, observing Lucian, thinking ahead, wanting to cover his own tracks if at all possible. He had only assisted Prebble in recent years. He had only received one payment each time, not an annual sum to keep him quiet. He had no idea that Prebble was earning £10 per plot per year; about how much was that a year? For the moment he would let Prebble sink in the mire, leave him to wrestle it out with the rector, wait his chance.

Prebble had fallen silent now. Lucian was attempting to sum up.

"I need to caution you, Prebble. This is an extremely serious business. I must see Mr and Mrs Summers at once, and assuming that only Mr Mathews knows (Prebble nodded) I must see him. I then have to contact the archdeacon and take his advice. For your part you must tell nobody, nor you Mr Burton. I need a full record of every single plot that you have reserved. I need to know that it is fully correct and totally up to date. I need to know who is currently paying you £10 a year. I need to know how much money you personally have taken over the years. And furthermore, I need to know that what people have paid for has indeed been done. Do I make myself clear Prebble, I must know that there have been no previous muddles? Have you lied about mistakes in the past? Have you ever dug up the dead before or is this the only occasion?"

Prebble fell to his knees. Lucian watched him with alarm. There was a long silence, observed by Burton, when verger and priest stood as if in effigy. Then Prebble began to weep. Huge, bulging bursts of wailing coming from the body, now spreading, fully prostrating on the reception room carpet. Lucian stood observing this extraordinary activity but uttering no words and doing nothing to help.

Burton stood up and spoke sharply. "For heaven's sake man, help him. Do your duty as a priest!"

Lucian looked at Burton and then at Prebble, who was now throwing himself about on the floor, still face downwards.

Both Lucian and Burton bent down to roll him over. As they did so Paula came into the small room with a tray of coffee, in time to see Prebble catch out for Lucian's throat with both hands screaming out, "Help me. Help me! Don't leave me now Rector! Help me!" Just in time to see a man she did not recognize raise his fist and strike Prebble senseless.

13

Peggy Newson was preparing to speak to a local history society that met each month in Newton Abbot. She was well aware that these gatherings were far more than respectable exchanges of information. Those who gathered had the advantage of education or retirement or both. They could ferret out a problem or tease out an error like a classroom of most gifted pupils. As individuals they were still reserved, but the collective pressure of their separate specialisms was impressive even to visitors from the university. They had recently had a disastrous evening listening to a lady from America talking about 'What America Means to Me', talking away like a frantic witch and showing them not slides of America but photographs taken during her initial months in England. They were all absurd, brash images of cafés and harbours and distant churchyards and, oddly, a number of views of public toilets that this exasperating woman called 'comfort stations'. Her ideas about America were equally nonsense.

Peggy Newson was struck with the idea of talking about sanctuary because it seemed to encompass so much of her own interest and research. The idea of a place that could become separate from any other building or use of place. The idea of consecration being advanced to this degree. The concept of God's judgement as a force to outreach any other sense of order. It was both naive and hugely complex. But where did the idea really come from? Who brought it to these isles and why was such a mystical notion acceptable? Was it even perhaps one of the longest active superstitions, or had all the television reportage of recent military encounters banished it? Did bombing Coventry and Vietnam and cheap American films take away finally all the rights of such a place of magic? But then wasn't she herself being naive? Had sanctuary ever really worked? Had it ever been real rather than a complex cheat? Wasn't it the few most famous cases that suggested glory instead of the misuse of a deity's domain?

She spent a good deal of time recalling the data, then the detail, and then the meaning itself. But how could the elements be reported, the magic and the meaning and men's minds?

The right of sanctuary was universally recognized from earliest times. The Old Testament cited the Hebrews' six Levitical cities of refuge. The Greeks and Romans attached a similar sanctity to their ancient temples and when the Empire became Christian, Roman law recognized the use of Christian churches as places of sanctuary. In Saxon England the laws of King Ina and of King Ethelbert likewise recognized the right of a murderer to take sanctuary in a church; 'and there to be entirely secure so long as the murderer stayed within the church'. King Alfred, in his code of laws, laid down conditions under which the fugitive might remain within sacred precincts and the maximum duration of his stay. He must not take any arms with him into the church. Watching to prevent his escape was the duty of the township or of the pursuer. The church authorities were only required to provide him with food.

She wondered what the real intentions were behind this idea, what the laws and codes were meant to create and for what reasons; but even more what it meant in the mind of the criminal or murderer who had put himself under divine protection. But was it really protection or a more sophisticated idea of placing one's guilt beneath the eye and mind of God, an admission and recognition thus later making the penalties less horrific, even the loss of life? Wasn't this some sort of gateway to God rather than an escape? Wasn't it really a true declaration, direct to God?

These sanctuary rights continued to be an important feature in the life of the people during the disturbed centuries following the Norman Conquest and throughout most of the Middle Ages. Every consecrated church and its graveyard had a limited sanctuary right for forty days for any refugee who sought it. Certain privileged churches and abbeys were given permanent and life-time sanctuary rights, the limits of which might extend as far as a mile and half from their doors.

Heavy penalties were prescribed for the violation of the rights of sanctuary within the limited period of forty days. There were dramatic occasions when the parson of a parish would stand guard at his church door with the elevated 'host' in his hands to prevent a pursuer continuing to chase therein. But after forty days had expired the fugitive had either to abjure the realm and take oath to this effect, or he must leave his place and state of sanctuary and surrender himself for legal trial, if his prosecutor could not otherwise be satisfied.

If his choice was to abjure the realm, he would set out from the church clad in sackcloth with a cross in his hand. He had to reach an appointed port within a specified time. He there boarded the first ship sailing overseas. Many innocent as well as guilty men escaped a gallows death by these means. The journey overseas meant a new life, but the concept of the death of the old ways was brutally real.

Atheists, professed, could not expect such understanding nor any who had committed sacrilege, but other than this there were no exceptions and dragging a man out of sanctuary was regarded as a sacrilege or profanity itself.

During the fourteenth and fifteenth centuries the right of sanctuary was jealously maintained. John Wycliffe and the Lollards advocated its suppression but in vain.

During the reign of Edward II even the Bishop of Exeter was forced to fly for sanctuary to St Paul's Church, London, although he was unhorsed and stabbed as a traitor before reaching it.

It was not until the Reformation that sanctuary suffered great curtailment and it was not abolished by law until the reign of James I. Even after this period English criminals fled for sanctuary across to the Continent where they were entirely safe.

Peggy Newson wondered what was cost in the crude understanding of men when you could not run to your God to escape human revenge or even honest punishment. And was this symbol so much understood, so taken advantage of, that it had to fall? Wasn't it one of the most amazing images and concepts in all religious experience, a massive measure of Christ's loss for man's sins, a space in the agony of sin and disputation and penalty given by the god direct? Perhaps it was the very splendour of the thing, the directness, that led not only into not disrepute but direct dispute with the earthly lords? Perhaps this magic was too much a trick and could no longer be tolerated?

But then all of this made the eight year sanctuary of one Richard, a deaf and dumb man, even more amazing. She recalled the deaf and dumb murderer who had taken sanctuary in the village church for eight years. It was an extraordinary thing. Why had the villagers agreed to feed him for so long? What was this amazing concept of sanctuary. Finally the man had agreed to be taken to Sherborne Abbey where he was provided for during the rest of his life. There was surely some hidden truth within this story, she thought, something about ordinary knowledge facing the cruel necessity of the State, or was it something quite different, was the kindness itself born out of fear? What special case was made to the Abbot of Sherborne and why was this man not sent to cross the ocean? What had it to do with his loss of hearing and speech? And what was it preventing her from finding a satisfactory account of this one man's life? The Diocesan Library, the card index, the hours of wading through papers and tracts led to nothing of significance. Was it because of the lack of speech, the low order of a deaf and dumb person, or the nature of his crime, or some mystery of coincidence and hidden consequence, to be kept hidden all these years? Was there nothing to be said or too much to be kept hidden? Was the secret about a person or persons unknown?

Would the local history society appreciate a mystery, unsolved; was this the sort of thing they wanted to spend their retirement resolving? Was it history or a game'?

14

Mrs Waley had insisted on Lucian returning to discuss the idea that was lodged so firmly in her head.

"The sheela does not belong here. It should never have come here. It was one of my husband's odder ideas. It needs to return to a place of worship and I want that to be here, in this parish. But I can see that you have a problem, Rector; please tell me what it is."

Lucian was unsure how to begin. He had talked with Peggy Newson, anticipating some dissention on the grounds of it not belonging here. He had hoped to hear her propose that it be returned to its original site or at least in that geographical and therefore historical vicinity. But Peggy Newson had appeared more amused by the proposition than seriously concerned.

"What is the point of it wherever we place it?" she had asked. "If we can in fact trace its last siting it may well be that it did not originate from there. There are several pieces in our own church that come from other churches and even stones removed from pagan sites. It is how these things are regarded and used that matters. They are not items of art after all. They are meant to mean, to be real, to be used."

Lucian wasn't sure what she meant. Did this old lady who kept the village history store up other things? Did her knowledge take her into other realms? How could a sheela be used, be real? It was surely purely a reminder of the ancient past. a symbol, no more and no less. Surely other villagers wouldn't perceive it in another way? Perhaps Peggy Newson was entirely the wrong person to advise him.

"The sheela is timeless, harmless, even innocent. It would be wrong to place it in a museum. I agree with my husband's view in that respect. No, it needs to be outside, in a place of spiritual significance, displayed on its own or placed in a niche. It won't look out of place I assure you."

"But it won't be understood," said Lucian, "it will surely cause upset. Either we will be accused of introducing some pagan curiosity or accused by the purists of stealing and displacing an ancient artefact or worse."

"Worse; whatever do you mean?" Mrs Waley asked.

"An earth mother, some part of pagan genius, an image that goes beyond an image. What will the village lads make of it I wonder!"

"Perhaps you need more time, Rector, but not too much I hope. I would feel really quite upset if you were to reject it but plainly that has to be your decision. What I do ask is that you don't take too long and that you do tell me the reasons for your rejection if that is what you choose to do. In any case I need to know what you personally believe, whether it is your voice or that of simple village people or the faint hearts of the church council. I am not prepared to take a simple no for an answer, there must be reasons."

"'Of course, you deserve that; I promise not to take too long," said Lucian; "why don't I say a month? There are a few people I need to refer to before finally making up my mind."

"May I suggest a name?"

"Of course, Mrs Waley."

"Then ask Peggy Newson," proposed Mrs Waley, "she has a feeling for the past, the way our time and past time mingle. She has an extremely strong sense of time as eternal returning rather than history being a record of retreat, the past, what is over and only once to be. Let her advise you about our sheela. Would it be totally a bad thing to shock a few worthies, to stimulate some debate, to get a few people thinking about images and stones and carvings as actual objects rather than solely symbolic. You know, I hate it every time I hear about 'church art'. It's like the Bible as literature, the scriptures as poetry, God as art. Are you aware of that, Rector? Are you prepared to perpetuate it?"

Lucian, haunted by Mrs Waley's challenge, let the image of the sheela flit in and out of his daytime thoughts. He found her persistence amusing, or was it less innocent, deliberate in some way, an old woman's rebellion against composure and certainty? Was she trying to roar off conformity, the certainty of the last years of her life? How could a small stone effigy do this?

And yet its power was strong and Lucian was unsure what to do with it. Easy enough to decline her offer, to give a reason or no reason. Easy enough to consult the church council, to get their dissent, and yet did he want to risk their dissent, to go through the convolutions of church politics, to annoy and risk their misunderstanding. Why not leave Mrs Waley to find some other recipient, some more suitable site, or better still why not get her to return the sheela to its original site?

But none of this satisfied Lucian. Didn't he actually want to cause something of a stir? Didn't he actually look forward to the taking of sides, the stating of positions? Perhaps to distract from other matters such as the illegal removal of babies from graves. Perhaps to distract himself from Paula's silences. Perhaps to conceal from himself the banality of a future without challenges and the stating of positions, the dreadful drone of ceaseless calm.

Sometimes the sheela came as a glimpse, a flurry of an image in the head, more than a day dream. The sheela in some shade of green with its grin and gripping fingers and then moonlight making it even more powerful, the stone less stone than real flesh, the creature more animal. Or the idea of its noise came to Lucian; noise of dark laughter, suggestive, impulsive. Or the idea of its smell came; something of blood and sweat and erotic pleasure and yet stale in its ancient fertility. Or the idea of some ancient animal flashed in and out; an animal playing with itself, perverted. Somehow incestuous, somehow associated with deep water that lay waiting, stagnant, colour of dead nettles.

And when Lucian considered where it might be placed, which exterior wall or which part of that wall, he was again uncertain, unsure about what sort of game he were guilty of. Should be perhaps experiment, say nothing but have it placed at the base of the wall near the porch and see just who noticed and await their comments? He would judge its reception before finally saying yes or no to Mrs Waley. Perhaps that was a way out. Peggy Newson would surely approve of this action; history as the meaning in present peoples' minds.

15

The appeal of the sanctuary in the church, the story of one Richard who in 1232 killed and ran for cover, banging his head against God's grace. This was now creating a firm existence in Peggy Newson's mind. She couldn't get into it easily. She needed to research and catch the coils of ancient light, beginning with the man himself. But it wasn't a search through pages, texts, parish records, it wasn't this that obsessed her. She began her search not with research but by thinking herself into the image and being of the man; his soul, his sense, his tension of survival, his stubborn virtue.

He stared into the terrible dark place searching for light. Sometimes he lay on the floor staring up at the roof wondering if God was really hovering on the other side. One Richard, a deaf and dumb man, who had killed a John Baldwin and now took sanctuary in the church for no less than eight years.

Sometimes he lay beneath a window letting light fall onto his face but not his body, as if this robe of brilliance would cleanse the memory of murder.

"Are you God?" he asked the light, the roof beams, the scented darkness, the coldest winter stone, the carvings in wood, the drenching sweat of summer, the small creatures running from corners or trapped in web, the corpses of dead birds who had starved to death, even rain that came in during storms. "Are you God to thunder at me?" he asked in his head.

Eight years of this. Fruit, meat and water from the villagers before they got tired of him and appealed to the Abbot of Sherborne to take him out of sanctuary. Eight summers when he sensed the voices distant outside and wondered if he should creep out at night simply to stand beneath a tree, smell fresh red soil, feel the true night wind calming his bones. Almost eight winters with no sight of snow, gabbling within his rags in the cold church with ice windows and the priest sometimes kicking him out of the way.

"Are you God?" he roared in one of the great thunderstorms, the lightning leaping like a jinxed creature, God's brain going crazy, the wind like a howl from earth's mind. "Are you God coming to thump me down to bone?" he raged in his soul.

He was at times ill. No physician came to him. Were they poisoning him? Were they doing him down? He lay in stone silence with a hedgehog that had somehow got in and was company for him until it died. On Sundays he kept to the back. During the week he lay around wherever he liked although he knew there were complaints. He could sense their doubts.

For eight years Richard hid away with a changing God, a chanting God, a torturer of limbs, a freezer of dreams, a fat old thing that never let him be.

"Are you God?" he asked, when the pain in his head was terrible for entire days, "is it words that will release me? Am I therefore doomed?"

And it was surely words, the words in books and chant, the priest's words and what the people said. "God give me words in my mouth," he screamed in his head, "give me the power of speech."

And then again he sometimes considered what God's laughter might sound like.

She began a poem; eight lined, tight little stanzas. It was, however, too tight. She let it flow into prose again.

She was aware of Wheldon's phrase 'In time one mingles the fact of any message with the fiction of one's interpretation of it'.

What was fable? What was the light and truth that outshone the detail? Was it always the echoes one heard and remembered?

Finally she began to place it down in one concentrated piece called 'Seasons for Richard the Dumb'.

I
He did not know where to put
his bones, his mind, his light;
for there was light, had always been
this beginning of hope. Earth cracks
into new days, old night collapses
and tall day climbs: day keeps
on making wonders, day brings out
green ideas so that death is held.

II
Seeing that they spoke to him
when he was so young, wanted to
warn him; kicked him, screamed,
beat into his soul; caught in the
centre of their curses and their smiles;
gobs of spittle and smiles; a fat
priest who looked down on him with
tigers in his smiles.

III

Better to stay in the corners, then.
Better not to come out to their claw
talk then. Clutch in the corner, the
stone edge, the shadows. Pick up meat,
heat, anything you can. Let the doubts
dribble and if they don't kill you
then exist, just exist. The green world
survives in a speechless field.

IV

He, motionless, set in shadows now, would
still get the running stench, the hunted fear,
falling into fields and woods and out across moors
as boys chased, men chased, horses with huge faces
broke down upon his secret places. They beat him,
held him beneath water, spat into his eyes, broke
his dreams. Sometimes, still heavy, ran until
the silent church froze his sweat.

V

What could the priest say to him without his
hearing, without the forms of speech? Was it these
men who told him of the force of sanctuary? He
could not have simply sensed it. Did such men as
priests lead him into this, their robes giving him
clues, authority? Somebody must have informed him,
or something, so that he made it to this church, or
was he brought here? After the murder was there a
chase, a hunt, or some enchanting system of cloaks
and dark journeys and hands helping him?
        But what could these men, or one particular
priest, have said in some form? Images of a cold
God who would not move to punish a dumb man. Images
of laws that could be withheld. Images of God's
trust outstripping the small identity of revenge.
        And what could Richard the Dumb do with this
speech, this host of hands helping him escape,
this place of stone silence and effigy and other
people's ceremony?
        Weeping in the poor, slobbering dark in winter.

Lying, wishing for fresh air, in August when the
very walls should have fallen back to flowers,
fields, perhaps even sea.

Richard the Dumb with bloody ghosts wrecking
his dreams and black angels spitting things he
could not hear and the drum of doubt still there,
despite his deafness, within the pulse, his memory.
his bone
But what, beyond all this, did the priests say
to themselves and to their congregations?

VI
There was one man they paid to feed him. He did
not like this man. He supplied water and vegetables
and some meat. When this man did not come his
woman came and it was she who sometimes spat in the water,
making sure he witnessed it. When she did not come
he imagined that the younger man was their son and
that he had urinated on the mess that was slopped
before him. But he consumed it all.
    The man who was paid to feed him never stayed
long but the woman sometimes stood nearby. She
stared at him with her filthy gob opening and
closing like a trap. She had few teeth and her hair
was white and if he didn't come out for his
food she went round the church bawling out for him.
He sensed her ridicule, her venom, her awful poison.
He saw her filthy feet deliberately kicking the water
pot over.
    And when the food never came at all, or when
the son served up a plate of earth and straw, or when
he found a toad mashed into the mess, he learnt
not to look up at their faces.
    When they threw a bucket of water over him
he kept his eyes down. When the son pushed him,
kicked him, ripped his hair back and screamed into
his face he wished he was blind as well.

VII

When there were services he kept himself hidden
under a pew in a far corner, although they knew he
was there. They all knew.He curled himself up
unless they had locked him in the small room above
the bells. Then he could feel the bells swinging like
huge animals beneath him. He could feel the floor
shaking. Sometimes he was left there all night.
No woman and no man and no son and no food. He
curled up into the tightest ball, clutching his
rags and bones until he became a stone.
He learnt how to do this. He was good at becoming stone.

VIII

In the real world priests understanding the sentence
of sanctuary; the farmers in the congregation uncertain
about the murderer in their midst; the farm children
told never to go near the church at weekdays; the
gravedigger always believing that Richard the Dumb
watched his deep digging, his preparations for
departure; the gentry not coming to this particular
church or not knowing much or anything at all about
Richard; the carpenter who came to replace two pews
talking to Richard as if he were simple and never
knowing that Richard was deaf; a lady from London
coming once to see the creature for herself and
being repulsed by his stench; complaints;
some dreams; some letters exchanged; some suggestions
that he be moved somewhere else; a doctor coming
to see if Richard's fever was going to kill him;
the bell ringers chasing him about for fun; sometimes
a gang of drunk men coming to the locked door to
 bawl for him to come on out; Richard dreaming of
the dreadful details of the murder. The details
change; they dither, they dash about, they deny,
they pull him into despair. Once a woman with a
very lovely face giving him a coin that he could
not spend; his staring at the carving of the pig;
the pig once or twice smiling back at him; his
dream of the pig carrying him off across white fields
and white villages and white forests down to

the white sea; his toe nails giving him a great deal of
trouble; his watching the small creatures running
about the church in their own real territory.

IX

He, sad, closed-down, lost, helpless, alone, watched
the priest and other people observing four men
getting the coffin into the ground. He recognised
the gravedigger and his brother but not the other
men. In his silence he observed, clutching at
the window to keep his view. The cold rang through
his rags and again hunger bit at his stomach. From
the darkness of the church the snow was brilliant.
One of the children was crying as the coffin went
down into cold earth. The priest clutched a bible
but didn't read from it. His mouth was moving as
it always did. Richard yet again wondered where
these people had come from, whose death it was, from
what cause, what house would they go back to? And
when they had all gone, he stayed staring as the snow
gathered its cloak over the mound of earth. It was
slowly creating the shape of a human body. The body
was underneath, in its coffin, but the shape on top
was now like a human shape. Shadow and death.

X

When he was very disturbed by the murder, the
detail real, all of it coming back, Richard the
Dumb sat waiting for the carving of the bird to
move again. He knew that it sometimes did this,
at night or just before dawn. He could see the
wings move a little and the dark wooden eyes
looked wet. When daylight grew it would not
be like this at all. He would not be afraid then.
He would stand nearer to the carved bird then and
see that it was only a carving and reach out to
feel the wings. Sometimes he stood by the carving
and hunched down and lifted his arms like heavy
old wings and imitated the bird moving in a circle,
very very slowly. His feet would plod about, slowly,
very deliberately, as if trying to get a more secure

grip. He moved his head up and down as though it bore
a big beak. He sensed the weight of the beak stuck
right in the centre of his head, in fact it was the
head entire. He moved the heavy beak from side to
side. Sometimes he waddled down the aisle with wings
lifted and from his chest there came a low warble,
a hunched scream of air. He felt the vibration of
it only, very deep within him. He liked this bird
being. But in the dark or early dawn it always
began in fear, a sort of anger, a strange disturbance
that worked itself into this recreation. Over the
years this activity became far more than a game, a
fear to conquer, a fear to defeat, a way of growing out
to greet and then defeat it. It became important.
He lay down dead as the bird sometimes. He hunted about
the filthy pews as the bird sometimes. He stabbed
at the dust and performed little jumps in the air.
 The game grew. But when it was so dark, before
he became the bird, it was a terror to him. It was
impossible to ignore. He couldn't block it out by
pretending, keeping his eyes shut. He was always
drawn into it. He believed in the bird.

16

"Please be seated and then I'll very carefully explain the purpose of this little gathering," said Lucian, aware of his nervousness and of the tension already building in the room.

Paula had served everyone coffee as they arrived, but this had done nothing to reduce the hostility and fear. Fred Summers and his wife were the first to arrive, then a distressed Mr and Mrs Mathews came into the room and insisted on sitting as far away from the Summers as possible. Finally Prebble and Burton joined them, both refusing the coffee offered by Paula.

Lucian hoped that Paula might stay but when she speedily departed Lucian didn't delay in outlining the purpose of the meeting.

"Nobody else is coming this evening and nobody else has been informed about the nature of the matter. It is up to now totally confidential. What we may be able to achieve this evening will, I hope, mean that it can remain this way. All I seek is your agreement, with me and with each other and then the matter can be resolved and no further action need be taken. Now then – "

"Now just wait a minute, Rector," broke in Brian Mathews, "I believe I heard you right but our twins right now don't lie in the grave we paid for, we reserved, and furthermore your verger, Prebble here, he's guilty of a crime and he could be taken to court."

Prebble reared up but Burton restrained him.

"Mr Mathews, I know how you and your wife must feel but I do beg for patience," said Lucian, again doing his best to keep control. "If it is a matter of law then none of you stand in a good position. The fact is you are all in the wrong. The payments of money, the reserving of graves, the removal of bodies is all totally wrong. Now please consider this: if any of this gets to a court it will not go well for anyone."

"Do you include yourself in that statement, Rector?" asked Mr Summers.

"Yes, certainly I do. I have to take some responsibility for Prebble's action over the years. I should have checked the official record from time to time. I might have questioned some of the sites chosen if I had been more diligent."

"So what do we do now?" asked Burton. "What's the purpose of this meeting? What's done is done and I don't see how we can change anything."

"Oh don't you, indeed!" exclaimed Brian Mathews. 'Well let me tell you, for a start we want our twins properly buried again, in the spot we chose and paid Prebble for. That's what has to happen for a start!"

Lucian wondered whether it might not be better to let the two men rage, to let all those assembled express their fears and tensions. Equally he wondered about his wisdom in calling the meeting. Did he really imagine that he could avoid contacting the archdeacon, informing the church council, and finally calling a public meeting. Would any of these people, seated now in tight silence, be able to yield, to think broadly, to consider their true and long-term position?

It was Susan Mathews who finally broke the silence. "I don't see the point of causing any more distress. Our twins were properly buried; it was all done properly by you, Rector. When they were moved, when that happened, I am quite sure God saw it and knew what was going on. Now they are buried a few yards away. All you have to do, Rector, is bless that ground and nothing else needs to be done so long as this whole business stops here. Somebody has to tell all those other people who've paid that the grave bagging is over. When that's done all this trouble will be over."

"What about our payments?" asked Mrs Summers. "What about paying £10 a year for years? Who's going to sort that out?"

Lucian looked at Prebble who appeared to be frozen to his seat. Burton flashed daggers at him.

Lucian saved him. "It must be made perfectly clear that there will be no further payments and no more grave bagging and equally clear that no money can be paid back. I understand that this foolish practice started before my time and before Prebble's time so Prebble cannot be held solely responsible. He is guilty for his part in it but then all who paid are guilty. If they had wanted to reserve grave plots they should have used the official system and applied for a faculty. By avoiding the official system and seeking to get what they wanted on the cheap they have offended. Anybody who has any part in this is therefore guilty. However, if you force my hand, if you persist in wanting repayment or any other sort of revenge I will be forced to take the matter to higher authorities. The entire church council and the archdeacon will learn of it and there will be a public enquiry and all that will expose the entire village to media attention. Is that what you really want?"

"We want peace and our twins need their new grave blessing," said Susan Mathews.

"Yes; that will be enough," said Brian.

"And you, Mr and Mrs Summers; do you agree?"

After a pause they agreed and left the rectory together. Lucian returned to the room to face Prebble and Burton. It was Burton who spoke.

"What happens now, Rector? Is that it? Who's going to explain about their being no paying back of money?"

"Prebble is," said Lucian. "It's the only way it can be done. Every single person needs to know. Every single person. I want to see every shred of the grave bagging destroyed, whoever paid and however much they have paid over the years. Is that quite clear, Prebble; is it?"

Prebble appeared to be incapable of speech. Burton helped him up and out.

Prebble stared and stared at his notebook. It contained ,elaborate plans of the churchyard with the official record of reserved sites in blue and his own system of bagged plots in red broken lines. There was a numbering system relating to payments to date.

At the rear of the book there was an accounting system made over the years by himself and his predecessors. It added up to almost a hundred people paying their £10 each year, some of them more than that if they had their eyes on two plots.

Prebble sweated heavily, drew in breath heavily, exhaled noisily, the saliva collecting at the edges of his mouth, biting the edge of his lip, chewing over the facts. He had taken in thousands of pounds. He couldn't possibly pay it back. He would have to inform all these people that they had wasted their money. He would have to call in person on each one. He would have to or risk going to court.

He now considered bluffing his way out of the mess. He could tell the rector that he had ceased the practice, had told all concerned, that all would now be well. The rector would have to believe him. He would make sure that certain of them were prepared to lie if asked direct, should the rector decide to check. Surely he could persuade some of them. And then, carefully, slowly, he could start the system up again and keep bringing in the cash. It was an advantage to the people. They wouldn't have to apply for a special faculty. All that time that it took. All that uncertainty. And it would be a lot cheaper. Should he perhaps reduce it to £5 for a whole, or £5 after five years? Or should he even raise it as the risk to him was greater? Perhaps he could use the threat of exposure to his advantage now. £10 for five years, then £5 for another five, then perhaps it could be free.

Prebble's greed consumed his caution, his fear. He began to relish the idea of a bluff, of double-crossing the rector, of maintaining his control. The relief is not having to see all those people and expose himself to their threats. They would surely threaten him. They would surely blame him. They would surely demand their money back–

Prebble's mind raced. One moment he saw an advantage, the next a problem: the next greed took over, the next fear returned. The one constant was that he had never started this, it had been handed down, it was not his fault. The system advantaged the people. It had only failed to work this once.

But could he trust the Summers, the Mathews? Could he trust the rector to trust him? Would he carry out spot checks? Would he demand Prebble's book be inspected and then destroyed?

He had never lied to the rector before. He had made sure that he knew his place. He had protected God's house from fashions, fads, modern ideas, mad men with crazy changes in mind. God knew this. God knew his purpose. God trusted him. Surely if God had not approved He would have smote him down. He had seen him digging the babies up. He had seen what he and Burton were doing. Surely he would have stepped in then?

But God had seen him and let him continue. God must have had a reason. And now God wanted him to stand up to the rector, keep control, stay on guard. All these figures, all this money meant very little in terms of God's love, His trust, His higher intention. God wanted him to do all this and keep doing it.

Prebble's certainty grew like a sunrise. It warmed him and then heated his imagination. He would lie to the rector. He would not let the people down. He would somehow deal with the Summers and the Mathews and Burton. He would need to tell Burton. He must tell him and use the man. Burton could protect him. Burton might even come up with an idea of his own. Burton would also be God's servant. Burton would have to start coming to church. Burton could do all sorts of little jobs and help him keep control, watch out for the rector, etc.

Prebble was smiling now. He heard God's banjo playing in his head; The Old Rugged Cross, Onward Christian Soldiers, Jerusalem.

17

Lucian blessed the new grave with Susan Mathews in attendance. It was a brilliant light that fell upon them. There was no sense of guilt in the act. It was a peaceful setting down, a settling, a pact, a promise to God and by God.

Afterwards Lucian prayed alone in the church. Again a sense of relief poured in on him. God's grace was here, his settlement, his resolution. Lucian felt uplifted, whole, stronger.

Prebble had promised to cease his mercenary practices. Prebble had vowed never again to take the law into his hands. Prebble had retreated into quiet obedience, working harder to polish and clean and sweep it seemed, no longer coming up to interrupt Lucian's private prayers. Perhaps fear of exposure had really taught him a lesson in humility amongst other things.

Lucian prayed for the Mathews, the twins, Prebble, Burton, and then Paula. He prayed for his son and daughter-in-law and for Thomas the boy with whom he shared a secret, the fall from a tree. That seemed to have occurred a considerable time ago now, but it was a matter of a few weeks past.

Paula; how could he pray for his wife? How could he consider her properly, her needs, her fear, her deep distress?

He also prayed for Sidney. As always it was the ending, the lack of ending the fact that no body had been discovered and that it had to be assumed that Sidney had drowned with his friend whose body had finally come ashore in Wales.

No burial for Sidney except a burial in the mind. No place to lay a body or ashes but a part of the south Wales coast with the grey meat of the sea in winter and the dazzling azure of spring. And somewhere, to come ashore perhaps one day, Sidney's body. Held now in a deep, a silence, a lonely cold, a place totally unseen; a frozen time. What were the words for this? How did one pray into this? Was this God's voice again, his trick, his ridicule, his purpose, his question, his failing?

Each time Lucian attempted to pray for Sidney the deep sea swirl returned. It broke his determination, his sense, his need. The cold froze out God.

Paula, driving at speed to Wales again, taking a few days off again, asking

Lucian to forgive her again, seeing herself at the steering wheel as if she were a free levitating spirit looking down on a person called Paula.

"Look at me Sidney, driving away from my normal life again, my respectable subservient role, my little life of conformity.

Look at me not screaming, not howling, simply sitting in a room from time to time reading all your letters; cards; words; messages.

Look at me not loving your memory enough, demanding more. Not loving Richard and Maureen and Thomas enough. Not caring whether I truly love your father or not.

Look at my days in the huge rectory, in the church, in the parish, within the folds of my silences. I perform my small duties and take care not to offend and have nobody I can speak to.

And then, as now, I drive off for a few days to be alone, to be in Wales, to be nearer to whatever you have become.

Where are you Sidney? Where must I put your death?"

Paula at the wheel, seeing herself as a stupid ageing thing in the fast car, in the late afternoon, in the necessary diversion of yet another visit to Wales.

It was a diversion of course. There was no grave there, no proof of a body, nobody she knew, no special place such as a church or a memorial or the site of some happy event. Paula had only visited Wales twice in her life before Sidney's drowning, once on the way to Ireland and once, years before, camping in north Wales with school friends.

There would be, as always, no poetry to the place when she arrived, no beautiful vista, no symbolic scenery for her. The small bay would always be empty, devoid of sense, in no way attractive.

So why oh why must she return once or twice a year and alone?

"Look at me, Sidney; here again. I have nothing to greet your silences with but my own. Between the garden and church and meals and answering the phone and seeing your brother and his family and listening to your father and the voices of the parishioners and the keeping up of the huge house... I have nothing, nothing at all.

So I come here, here, to this bay, this place you probably have no memory of.

Memory. I speak as if you lived. I speak as if I knew where you were, as if contact were possible.

Look at me now, in this rain, in this impossibility, in this gesture, in this need.

I bury you in words that are not spoken, in hours when I am thinking of you, in dreams that visit during the day, in small scenes that locate my being, in rooms that have not heard your voice.

Sometimes I see the wife you never met, the cottage you did not buy, the family photograph you did not enter, the birthday card I cannot send. Oh look at me not looking too closely at the present because it cannot compliment the real past.

The words I do not use. The gestures I do not make. The hands I do not hold. Look at me not doing all these things.

The words not listened to with Lucian. The laughter not shared with Thomas. The letters, the letters, the messages on postcards buried in the garden, roaring from the dark hole, screaming from the silence.

For years you came into my night dreams and when I awoke the world was bandaged, wounded, broken-winged. In the dream your presence was golden, your voice reassured, your face was always wonderful. There was no hint of reality. There were no limits.

The doctor, the specialist, the friend, Lucian, the psychiatrist in his enormous room, the archdeacon, Maureen; you all came to me or I visited you. Your ideas were bandaged. Your kindness was circled with barbed wire. Your concern was like a very old painting."

Here, in Wales, a telephone call to Lucian, the same small hotel, the same metal music, a telephone call to Richard, a stray dog on the beach, a telephone call to God.

Will I stay long? Would I like Lucian or Maureen to join me? Is it really a good idea for me? Is it necessary? Is it real?

Lucian so quiet and patient. Our bandaged bond. Richard finding it hard to control his rage, contempt even. Maureen saying over and over it is understandable, obvious, quite sane.

The small bedroom. The tea-shop. The visitors already here. Freshly painted benches. The expectation of a new season. The car park attendant painting his small hut.

What do I say to the bright image, the beach balls and buckets, the postcard stands, the ice-cream signs? How do I disappear?

"Oh look at me, Sidney, floating between these realities and my own world, reaching out, invisible, not really here.

Not quite here. Not really in control. Not all here. A little bit deranged. Arranging what no longer exists. Gone in the head. A little bit off the rails. A screw loose. Somewhat lacking.

Until Lucian or Richard train down and pick me up and bring me back.

Their words falling like petals. The journey home revealing the real world, the images that have been kept waiting, the bandaged sun."

18

The wedding of Mary Symes to Phillip Taylor was going to be exceptional so far as Lucian was concerned.

Mary Symes was thirty-six and her parents had been in service at Barton Hall all of their married life. She had assisted at the primary school, first as a volunteer and in the last ten years paid an official ancillary rate. She was short, plain, quiet and nobody in the village had ever anticipated her marrying.

Phillip Taylor was the only son of the owners of Barton Hall, Major Ralph and Molly Taylor. He was restricted to a wheelchair and only a few in the village remembered what he had been like as a small and healthy boy before the illness that left him paralysed.

He had been sent to a special school and later trained as a librarian but increasingly he spent long periods at Barton Hall sick and in bed and gradually losing his independence. And naturally enough Mary Symes had begun to help her mother care for him as Molly Taylor herslf became ill and less capable. Phillip Taylor had to be fed, dressed, washed, exercised. It was a demand that increasingly galled all but Mary. And slowly her interest led to friendship and finally devotion.

The major was concerned with the future of his son. He saw in the marriage relief for his wife; he was in no way concerned that his poor son might be marrying beneath him. If this sturdy, reliable, sensible lass were prepared to take on a lifetime of increasing strain and restriction and act as a slave to his needs so long as he lived then so be it.

Lucian was impressed beyond words with both Mary and Phillip. Alone they were limited by their own natures as well as the strength of their parents. Together, as a couple, they were striking. The sight of them together in the village, their specific and detailed requests regarding the wedding service, the evident love and respect they held for each other, everything about their presence was impressive and positive. It was going to be a quite exceptional wedding so far as Lucian saw it.

When, as he had anticipated, there were some in the village who criticised such a union Lucian went out of his way to challenge such ignorance. What was it based upon; fear of deformed flesh, a failure to hear and see Phillip Taylor as an exceptional being, a simple refusal to accept such differences of class and upbringing now mixing in love. Lucian made it quite clear whenever the opportunity came that such a union would be extra blessed, an exceptional achievement, something to be wondered at in a truly positive way. This would be a celebration beyond the normal joy of weddings.

And so it seemed as the church filled up with villagers and many more members of the Taylor family and friends from Phillip's special school. A ramp was put down at the entrance to the porch so that those guests who also sat in wheelchairs could easily enter the specially decorated church.

The customary gathering of village women at the lych gate was much larger than usual and other villagers stood by the churchyard wall in small groups as the sound of hymns swelled from inside the church itself.

The service was unusually long because Mary had chosen so many hymns and an anthem for the choir and a sermon and Major Ralph read a lengthy passage from the New Testament and then a poem by John Clare.

And Lucian had toiled many hours with this particular sermon. As he rose to the small pulpit the faces he met confirmed his joy and his need to celebrate harmony and all that was positive in life and all that love could bring. It had after all been the full marriage service with no dispensations. Children might follow. Old age was possible.There was every reason to confirm every Christian expectation. Lucian therefore proclaimed the meanings of the marriage vows, the work that a real marriage required, the place of God and the church in this union, the special advantages that Mary and Phillip had. Lucian's sermon was indeed fervent and fine and positive and to Paula's mind, and one or two others, slightly over the top,

When the register had been signed the bell ringers began to give it their best and family photographs were taken in front of the porch. Many of those assembled became aware of the crowds of village folk augmenting the noise and as confetti flew huge bursts of cheering went up.

Phillip's best man and other male friends hoisted him up into the open carriage and the horse and trap began its journey to the reception at Barton Hall. The cars began to follow in procession, the villagers then went about their ways and Lucian returned to the church to tidy his papers and change before also making his way with Paula to the Hall.

He found her seated in the front pew just below the pulpit and immediately sensed her thoughts. He joined her and took her hand in his.

"For better or worse, Paula. A good marriage was made today and we still have a good marriage. We still have our health and each other and Richard and his family. We still have our faith and God's love to protect us. We still have years to go to achievements to enrich us and service to others. Oh Paula, if only you could feel this as I do, this expectation of good things."

"Oh yes, Lucian; yes I can see that you believe all of that. You are a good man. You are very strong. But we can't all keep up with you. We can't all be as strong. We need to pause and weep."

Lucian was astonished by such frankness. He let the silence of the church and the brilliant light of sunshine through stained glass govern the moment. The images and sounds of the recent service were also held there, and previous wedding services, previous promises before God, the pulse of vows.

Prebble and Burton could then be heard as they swept up the confetti. Both men were talking. Lucian could hear Prebble grumbling. "What's the point of it I ask you? That girl's going to be lumbered all of her life. She's a virtual slave."

Then Burton's voice, lower, more sinister. "Can't imagine what her parents were thinking of. That there girl needs what all women need and he ain't going to be much use. Fancy getting laid by a cripple."

Lucian, furious, rose to meet both men but Paula caught him by the elbow.

"Don't," she said, "don't try to stop them. It doesn't matter what they think; it only matters what Mary and Phillip think, and what they continue to think. Let those ignorant men stay ignorant."

"But it's my duty, Paula; it's my duty to break down such ignorance and stupidity. No, I must do it."

"Again, you are so strong," said Paula. "Whatever you say will only anger them."

But Lucian had already left the pew and was making for the door. Outside he found the two men still grumbling and apparently Burton was still going on about Phillip being incapable. They saw Lucian and fell silent. Lucian, still furious, was nevertheless careful in phrasing what he wished to say.

"I overheard you, I'm afraid. If you two insist on talking in the way you do people will overhear. I must say I'm amazed and ashamed by your extreme ignorance. Your comments are totally uncalled for, smutty and indicative of small minds. The two of you should be thoroughly ashamed."

"Is that a fact?" said Burton, "is that a fact? Who are you to talk going about marrying cripples to young village girls. Who do you think you are?"

Prebble, evidently afraid of the turn of events, nevertheless then felt forced to speak his mind as well.

"This has never happened in this village before, Rector; there's plenty who don't like it. That there marriage should never have taken place."

Lucian let a few seconds slip before responding. By now Paula had joined him and the two men were looking down, slightly ashamed.

"At least it was open, done in God's own house, blessed by the name of Jesus. At least it was honest and positive and hopeful. Not done, gentlemen, in the dead of night, not done for greed of money, not done secretly, and totally legal."

Burton made to respond but Lucian was determined to have the final word.

"And on that matter both of you appear to take me for a fool. Ah yes, I see I have struck a chord. I need to see you in the rectory, Prebble, tomorrow at three p.m. please, with your evil little book and a full explanation. Do you hear me Prebble? And you might as well bring Burton with you."

"Somebody's grassed on us!"

"Some bugger told him!"

Prebble and Burton, seated in the vast byre on Mrs Waley's estate.

"How could he know? Who told him?"

"More to the point, what are we going to do?" asked Burton.

The two men had walked over to the Waley estate directly after the rector's rebuke They were initially stunned by the rector's statement and command to report to the rectory. Walking through the fields on the brightest of afternoons had done nothing to assuage their fear, their anger, the hurt.

Inside the byre both men could begin to collect their thoughts.

"If he knows what we're up to," Prebble began, "that we didn't actually stop doing anything, that people are still paying me, he'll bring the archdeacon in. What's to stop him?"

"Something has to stop him. If that archdeacon comes in we're done for. We have to get back at him somehow,"

"Threaten him," said Prebble.

"Scare him off."

"We need some story to spread about, we need to start a rumour."

"Or catch him out. Get him to make a mistake," said Burton.

Clutched within the rays of light, surrounded by the farmyard litter and tea chests and boxes, the two men hunted in their heads for a way out. A trap. Some piece of poison. Some weapon.

It was Burton who made the first move. He got up and went to the back of the byre. Prebble couldn't see what he was up to. Burton was returning to him but holding something in his arms that was concealed under sacking cloth.

"Now then," said Burton, sweating heavily, "have a look at this. Tell us what you think of this." He grabbed away the cloth to reveal a small, stone, evil-looking deformity; a child-sized, chubby, crude thing with its cunt pulled right out. Terrible looking obscenity. Vile bit of ancient witchcraft. What was Burton up to?

"Don't you see; we place this in the porch, tonight. We put it there for everybody to see. We let people know the rector's gone off his head and put a bit of filth in the church. We tell them, see. We stir up a row and make sure the rector don't want no more problems. We write to the archdeacon and tell him there's a bit of filth in the church and it's all the rector's idea. We fit him up, see. We get him in so much trouble he won't want the archdeacon to get into the grave business. We make the rector so scared he thinks any more trouble and he's going to be sacked. See?"

Prebble still had his eyes fixed on the stone image, its vileness, its ancient wickedness. But Burton was right. They could fix this up in the vacant niche above the main door and tell people and get the rector into trouble. They wouldn't even go to see the rector. They would totally ignore the man. They would scare him rigid.

Then perhaps the man would go, leave, or be sent away. Better still be deprived of the living. A new man would come, some old fellow who Prebble could control. A nice, quiet old boy.

They could do it tonight. They could take the vile old thing out of this byre and get it in position and Burton could get a rumour going in the pub tomorrow mid-day.

"Guess what; Rector's gone potty. He's put a filthy bit of stuff in the porch for everybody to see. Dirty little figure with a pulled-out pin hole. Rector's gone round the bend he has!"

19

'History is not mirrors or windows or review. It is not letters and laws, legislations and tracts, the ins and outs of politics and powers. The history of men, buildings, nations, movements, emotion, concepts etc. is not the capturing of these things but as much the attempts to recapture, record, remember and evaluate against the contemporary for the sake of nothing. There is no point to history. There is no value whatsoever to it because so much is lost. History cannot be honest therefore it cannot be honestly assessed, recorded, evaluated. Even if history is not lies, it is not balanced, considerate, equal. It cannot possibly be but corrupt because of the manners, systems, means of its creation. It is partial, it is vague, it is retrospective, it is massively simplified, it is quite unlike any other function, fashion. Ah yes; its fashion is one of its weakest attributes. No history can come into being but by the foibles, dreams, doubts, dissentions of its creator, the historian. The historian naturally does not believe in foibles, dreams, doubts, dissentions. The man or woman, or more often groups, says here is the source material, here are some evidences, this is the context, these are the comparative details, and so now we pronounce this and this. History is therefore neither mirrors nor windows but a sense of what might be behind the shutters. It is coming across famous places on the days when the famous people have left. It is like pouring light onto a place that would prefer darkness. You do not get real light, you cast a shade or, worse still, you create shadows. History is not bunk, neither is it a bank of dreams. It is more like raiding an empty space and telling people about the significance of the search afterwards. History is therefore about the search, not the found; it is about the need to search rather than finding the drawer empty.'

Peggy Newson read all this, written very late one night with a mind full of wine and good Mozart still planting ideas in the night room. It was for that moment more exciting than the hut circle on Brown Heath, the carvings on pew ends at Braunton Church, the discovery of a Kistvaen in the Yealm Valley.

But even her words, her night room, her very ideas were suspect. She needed to talk about it, to escape it, to let it lift off the pages. It was too neat, too tight within words, still too tied down.

Peggy Newson left her papers, her texts, to stroll in the green dawn village. She needed the space of it, the soft noises of its awakening.

The sheela-na-gig, its vulva as big as her head, grinning with knees wide apart, now perched above the door to the church, the two men having gone away.

The sheela-na-gig with the light of moon falling across its form, the grin bigger than ever in the green and silver light.

The sheela-na-gig once more in a place of consecration, blessed effigies and stained glass images and stone symbolism.

A light wind now in the trees. An owl flying nearby. The vast green countryside almost visible. The church clock tick, ticking and striking the hours.

Deep in the sheela's spirit some ancient energy responding, growing, bulging, becoming again.

And as the dawn arrives the sheela changing shape, form, visage. The details redefined. The texture even changing.

The sheela a little smaller. The grin not quite so broad. The fat hands perhaps less livid. The erotic grimace reduced.

And first to visit the church that morning, not Prebble or Burton or Lucian but Peggy Newson, filled with ideas and poetry and propositions, coming into the porch and seeing at once the sheela.

"Oh my goodness; how utterly miraculous! How excellent! What a lovely idea as we begin to see the harvest appear!"

20

Lucian, furious with Prebble not turning up, eager to stay on top of the situation, playing his hunch (for indeed he had no proof of Prebble's deceit) decided to challenge the man outright and call in the archdeacon in order to discuss the verger and once and for all clear up the matter of the graves. One solution would be to give each person who had reserved a site through Prebble a faculty application and forget entirely about monies already paid to Prebble. The man could agree to leave of his own accord or be formally summoned for fraud and digging up an occupied grave and removing two infant bodies. Burton naturally would face the same or similar charges.

Lucian hoped to find Prebble in the church, no doubt accompanied by Burton. They would argue but Lucian would maintain control by the threat of legal proceedings. Prebble would have to yield. Quite apart from the procedures of both state and church, Prebble would have to face the wrath of his village friends, those who had paid him so much over the years. Perhaps the fear of mob attack would force Prebble to retreat. Lucian was even prepared to give the man two months wages to get out.

He found the outer gate to the porch already open and felt for his keys in order to unlock the main door. Then he saw the figure in the niche and instantly recognized it. Indeed, it looked quite well. Perhaps it could stay there. He wondered how it had got there. Perhaps Mrs Waley was somehow trying to force his hand.

He looked round to find Peggy Newson approaching.

For some reason he couldn't get the door to unlock. With Peggy Newson by his side and keen to tell him how much she admired his decision to place the sheela in the niche Lucian struggled with his keys but was forced to give up.

Shedding the enthusiastic Peggy Newson as politely as he could (why did she go on and on about the sheela? Why was this image so important to her?) Lucian made his way to Prebble's cottage to find nobody at home, or at least nobody prepared to come to the door.

He called at Burton's cottage and then guessed that the man would be already at work on the estate. Should he visit Mrs Waley and ask her about the sheela?

Lucian was considering this when yet again Peggy Newson came to his side.

"Rector, Rector; at last I've found you. I must speak to you."

"Could it possibly wait? I really am very busy just now. I'm trying to find the verger and..."

"That's it, that's who I've come about," said Peggy Newson, "it's about the verger. He's inside the church. He's locked himself inside. He says he's taking sanctuary."

Lucian, perched on a ladder, peering in through the stained glass, with Peggy Newson holding the ladder steady, could just make out the figure of Prebble inside. He was moving about the church, evidently barricading the doors. He ignored Lucian's calls and shouts although he must have been fully aware of them.

Later, with the archdeacon by his side, Lucian attempted to get Prebble to at least listen. He would not be harmed. The archdeacon understood and would sort everything out. He would not be charged with anything.

Lucian and the archdeacon withdrew for lunch. As Paula served salad they debated the best plan of action.

"At all costs we need to confine this," the archdeacon was saying. "We need to resolve this before news gets out and the villagers get to hear about it and somebody contacts the local press. But first of all we need to get into the church."

"It's not possible," replied Lucian, "if each door has been bolted from the inside then there's no way we can effect an entry other than by force. And even then it will take considerable muscle power!"

"Oh no; we can't have that. Under no circumstances. Either your man Prebble agrees to come out or we wait for him to give in. Let us remember it is sanctuary that he is claiming."

The archdeacon was adamant. Whilst he made some phone calls Lucian began to wonder where Burton was. No doubt having a pub lunch. Then he would return to the estate. Perhaps he should be contacted there. Could Burton be persuaded to help them in knocking some sense into Prebble? It seemed highly unlikely. Burton was the more cynical of the two in Lucian's opinion.

Arriving back at the churchyard both Lucian and the archdeacon were very surprised to find a crowd of villagers and Burton shouting from the front.

"Look at it, just look at it," he roared. "Calls himself a man of God and puts in this little bugger. Look at it, I ask you! The man must be off his rocker."

"For heaven's sake man!" shouted the archdeacon, "what on earth are you going on about? What's your name and why are all these people here?"

Burton wasn't easily put out of balance.

"Aha; two priests I see! Now then, who are you?"

"I'm the archdeacon and I demand some respect from you, Consider where you are man. This is hallowed ground."

Burton leapt at Lucian and standing imperiously against him wagged his finger whilst bellowing his offensive lecture.

"Right you are, my good Mr Archdeacon. Right you are. Now this good rector of ours has introduced into this hallowed place as you call it an evil, wretched, bewitched little idol of Satan. Look here! Look at this! Look up there above the door!"

The crowd surged forward as the archdeacon raised his head to the sheela. Lucian was by his side. As the two men stared up the crowd began to chant, led on by Burton.

"Dirty old devil, dirty little tart,
dirty old devil, dirty little tart!"

The archdeacon whispered something to Lucian before turning on the crowd. His clarity and firmness soon impressed even the loudest agitator.

"Now listen to me. First of all I sense that some of you have had just a little bit much to drink. Aha; that's so isn't it? Then let me suggest to you, not one of you knows why you've come here. I mean, what are you chanting about? This little image! This bit of sculpture! If that's so, if you really wish to object to this, then have a good look but higher up. Look; up there. Look at the gargoyles. Look at that ugly face over there. Look at that devilish creature above the downpipe. Have a good look why don't you! Now what on earth are you doing chanting about this poor little creature? Does one of you know its name? Eh? Cat got your tongues? Isn't there one of you who knows what it's called. Come on, you had a lot to say a few moments ago? Speak up now; what's it called? Eh?"

As the crowd fell silent it was Burton who the archdeacon was directly questioning. One or two village men were backing off, moving away, but the archdeacon was aggressively persisting in nailing Burton.

"Come on, man; what is your argument? Perhaps you can tell me the name of the object you hate so much and why you hate it? Come on; why have you led this silly demonstration?"

Burton was nonplussed, exposed, deeply hurt. But he knew that he was no match for the archdeacon.

"Ask the verger, Prebble, ask him," was all he could reply.

"That," said the archdeacon, "is very much my intention. And perhaps you can help us to bang some sense into his head."

"What do you mean?" asked Burton. "Where is he?"

"He's locked himself in the church. He says he's taking sanctuary there. Perhaps you can explain why he's behaving in this way. Perhaps you know more than we do Burton: it is Mr Burton isn't it?"

Burton made for the archdeacon but halted at the last second. With his face held close to the archdeacon's he issued his final threat. "You leave me alone, see. I don't know anything. You leave me be you bloody priest or I'll make you all regret it. I don't know a thing about Prebble, not a thing. He's mad I expect; mad as hell! You're all mad. I'm off."

When they had all gone Lucian and the archdeacon stood for a while in silence. Then dimly at first but growing they could hear Prebble's voice from within the church.

"You help me God! You help me keep them out God! Look, I'm going to give this place a nice old spring clean and then you and I can have a nice long talk. OK? A nice long talk. I've got so much to tell you. I've got my entire life to tell you about. I've got lots of good ideas.

21

Prebble, locked within his obsession, cleaned the brasses, dusted the pews, polished floor tiles, hoovered the altar carpet, polished the communion vessels, thoroughly cleaned the hymn book shelving, poked a long brush along the high window ledges, shook dust from the organ curtains, rearranged the pamphlet and magazine stall discarding old and faded and damp copies.

He worked for hours without stopping. He muttered messages to God. He clung to his task in desperation.

"God's house, this place. Got to keep it special for Him. No other place on earth like this. God's holy house. No noise here except for sacred sounds. No rushing about here. All ceremony and ritual and regulations. All ordered and special. No shouting here. All whispered and considered and peaceful. No arguing here. God's house. God's light. God's world. Got to get it specially clean now. Got to keep it right in here. Got to take sanctuary here. Got to keep myself here.

Lock the other world out. Lock that rector out. Lock that Burton out. Lock that obscenity thing out. Keep those words and accusations and look out. Keep the village out. Keep the ordinary out. Lock it out."

After many hours Prebble stopped and sat in a rear pew. He felt hungry but banished food from his mind. There was water from the vestry tap and he'd have to forget food.

The light was beginning to fade now. It was changing from the pink and green of stained glass to dark purple and brown. Soon it would be dark and he could sleep here. Sleep in God's silence, at the centre of his peace.

He fell asleep in the rear pew, slumped down, exhausted. For several hours he lay in peace before coldness and hunger woke him up. On waking he again banished the idea of food from his mind. If sanctuary meant starving then so be it. It was then that he knew he was not alone in the church.

Prebble suddenly crouched low, afraid, terrified. Had somebody somehow got in? Was it a policeman or Burton and somebody like Brian Mathews about to drag him out and beat him up and take him to prison and...

But where was this person? Prebble peered over the top of the pew to get a proper look. Nothing. Nobody. Oh but there, there it was; a man standing in front of the carved bird.

What man? How had he got here? Who?

Prebble, still terrified but curious, forced himself to observe. In the green light he could see a man he couldn't recognize, a man dressed in torn cloaks, a man from some other time.

This man, this figure, this image now reached-out to touch the bird, to feel its wings. Prebble, amazed, was now aware of a stench, an odour, a smell of something extremely old and decayed. Was it the man or the bird?

The man was still examining the bird but now he hunched down and lifted his arms like heavy old wings and imitated the movements of a big old bird. He plodded about, slowly, very deliberately. Then he began to move his head up and down, birdlike, as though his head bore a big beak. He moved his head up and down, from side to side, and then waddled down the central aisle as if he had become bird, with actual beak and wings and claws. Now he gathered momentum and lifted his wings and from his chest there came a long, low warble, a hunched up scream of air.

Now the bird began to hunt between the pews. He jabbed at the hassocks. he ran along the pew tops, he made small jumps as if he would fly up.

And the stench of the man become bird was more evident now. Prebble could sense the vile, ancient, stench of sweat and urine. He could see man and bird separate then unite again. He could hear both the man scream and the bird warble. He knew the stench came from both of them.

And now the bird, the man, the beast of them both, was gradually working its way back to where Prebble hid. The big bird was hunting, sensing him out. And the brain of the man must have sensed this too.

Prebble considered dashing to the door. Could he make it and pull back the bolts and heave open the door and escape? Would he be chased out into the churchyard and devoured by this creature?

Or should he stand up and face the creature and the man? Were they ghosts? Were they caught in some loom of time? Was he in fact imagining them?

Prebble was for a second or two convinced that this was so. If he could gather his courage, grip his fear and stand up surely the image would vanish? Whilst he hid, crouched down, the image was growing. He had to stand up. But no, no, he couldn't do it. He was forced down in cold fear, in terror, in the stench of cowardice.

The bird was closer now. The bird was bigger now. It was now only about ten pews away. It was too late to run for the door.

Prebble suddenly stood up and rushed in terror to the back of the church and grasped for the door to the tower. Throwing himself up the steps, the totally dark steps winding, winding up, he felt the freezing cold fingers of dread on his neck but somehow forced himself up and up and up until he reached the ringing chamber. He slammed the door shut behind him. He knew there was no key to the chamber so he began to stack some chairs against the door and then dragged a bookcase across to add to the barricade. Only then did he think of turning on the light.

The light made all the difference. The ordinary, dull bulb gave him exquisite relief. It was so simple. It was so real.

Prebble leapt now for a bell rope and began to toll. It seemed to him that the sound of the bell would never come and then, when it did come, it was so distant, so fragile, so weak. But he kept at it, he grasped the rope and heard the bell repeat and repeat and repeat until it fell with its huge and massive weight encasing everything beneath it, as it broke through wood and floor and gathered chaos in its frame.

22

I

Prebble falling, the light exploding, expanding beyond light,
the words in his soul imploding, clinging in a chaos,
the vocabulary of his being ravaging, ruining, ranting;

saw angels swinging through flames and breaking bells,
saw priests catapulted from smoking pulpits
caterwauling in their catharsis,

or stretched catgut tight, or wheeling between their screams,
the babble of their bile swamped by Bible blubber,
monstrous gargoyle grimaces, demon squealing; falling, falling.

Prebble falling between the lunges of black angel wings,
meshes of bat crap, smells ancient meat, the stench
of slavery, the gobs of demons,

hears babies roaring, the swearing of serpents,
and now feels his own body twisted tight and coiled
through the fat flesh and farting of the sheela-na-gig

whose buttocks imitate bosoms, whose genital gesture
derides him, and slowly sucks his entire body in,
grinding his senses, swallowing entirely his existence.

He enters the hole, the wound of it, the heat of it,
his body half in half out satisfying the demon lust,
his nausea ripped, his stomach spinning blood;

the sheela-na-gig now gradually consuming him entirely
before he is half in half out as she squats to eject him,
a human stool, Prebble the turd, caked in blood;

falling, falling again, aware now of his own screaming,
his own image inside the pit of bones and sluicing savagery,
the horned one and the bleeding-eyed one and the clawed one

roaring abuse by his side, falling in spinning space within him,
twisting with burning bone, with dead babies, with thousands of
hands that try to clasp, to close in, to grip.

Prebble falling past this existence, beyond the falling place,
the ground that must have killed him, the pain that
must have been there, the knowledge of no knowledge,

Prebble falling into the end of his time, the wound of his life,
the hole of his death, the bladder of being, is aware
of no end, no pain, no death, no intervention

as now falling, he is totally engulfed in each half second
of revulsion, terror, expectation, dread of dread,
the doom damning his being, flicking up confusion

and what was knowledge, what was faith, what was self
spinning into the scream, smearing all sense, ramming
his soul into the falling itself, locked into the arch of

falling, locked into the fusion of it, hearing within the
motion as his senses splatter and regroup and thrash
to destruction over and over, falling and falling .

If he could think. If he could for a second decide.
If he could begin to. Gather in. Start to. Try to.
Prebble falling totally disintegrates and reforms and

bloats into other bits of being. He is a tree stump
in a wilderness. He is a bird on a crag of ice.
He is a minute insect hunting a surface for escape.

He is a doubt in the mind of the saint who is drunk.
    He is a fever crawling up the woman's legs as she vomits.
        He is a cancer creeping round the brain of a priest.
            He is a rat.

II

Prebble is a rat, in a winter place listening to the hunters,
the noises from humans, the leap of curses;
his eyes narrow to green slits.

Prebble is a dog, in a winter place, in a building with no windows,
no doors, no ceilings. Above him the bats pour their shit;
he tastes the cold.

Prebble is a rabbit, in a winter place, its neck caught in a wire
that tightens, screws down his scream, fastens him to
his own pain, the agony of the certainty.

Prebble is a rook, in a winter place, the men, with guns
arriving now to finish him off. Clinging from the branch, upside down
hanging, as they shoot off each wing in turn.

Prebble is so small he cannot feel anything. He doesn't appear
to have a body. A vast eye looks at him. The eye
is a mile high, gleaming fat.

Prebble is aware that at any second the teeth will clamp,
the claws fasten, the jaws rip open. His brain will bounce
out like a small handbell.

III

Prebble, falling,
again falling,
tries to catch
hold on anything.
He might spit
back the rage,
scream out the
huge insult,
fasten his rage
and let it coil
into pain, pain.
If only there was

a pain, a tall
spike of it, a
huge spear of
it, a large gap
of hissing agony.

IV

The silence now
                as he continues to fall
past the voices he does not understand
                as he falls
Past the faces that stare back from bleeding glass
                as he falls
between stars and oceans and light rays
                as he falls
between oceans and grey beard waves and snow
                as he falls
between mountains and purple hills and ice crags
                as he falls
between whales and sharks and dolphins
                as he falls
between a huge hand holding an egg and
                a huge hand holding a coffin
                as he falls
between a net of words and boxes of silences
                as he falls
 between the sound of a scream and the sound of Mister Punch
                as he falls
between the faces of foxes and the faces of old men
                as he falls
between the face of Hilda White and Mavis Duke
                as he falls
between the faces of Lucian Fairbrother
                and
                Lucian Fair...

Prebble, lying on the ground, terribly hurt, crushed, destroyed, about to enter
death, can hear Lucian Fairbrother's voice, just hear it between sheets of huge
pain engulfing his blazing body. Can hear, just hear the priest comforting with

words. Words. Words. The light at the edges of the words just visible. The world just visible. The tiny world still there. Still here. Still now. The little universe still clinging to him. Still here. Just. Then out.

23

He looked down on Mrs Waley's gravestone, and on that of Peg Newson and other villagers he had known. He carefully hunted down the grave of twin babies as well but deliberately did not stay there long.

Inside the church the same ancient signs and symbols greeted him, as if even the greatest moments of his life were simple, limited.

He noted his name inscribed on the list of past rectors and on departing looked up at the small figure in the niche above the door. A very simple stone carving of a virgin and child looked down upon all who came into this porch. It was another quiet reminder of the gentle moving on of things.

At the rectory gate Lucian could see a driveway that looked very much the same, and yet he knew that the present rector lived in a small, modern house and that the former rectory was now a guest house. And Mrs Waley's house was a training centre owned by the county education authority.

Lucian walked a little way up the drive and then veered to the left. Carefully he made his way through evergreens and old bushes trying to find what had been the tree house. After half an hour he was forced to give up.